THE STILLWATER TRAGEDY

Thomas Bailey Aldrich

1ˢᵗ WORLD
LIBRARY
Literary Society

The Stillwater Tragedy

Thomas Bailey Aldrich

© 1st World Library – Literary Society, 2005
PO Box 2211
Fairfield, IA 52556
www.1stworldlibrary.org
First Edition

LCCN: 2004195681

Softcover ISBN: 1-4218-0495-6
Hardcover ISBN: 1-4218-0395-X
eBook ISBN: 1-4218-0595-2

Purchase *"The Stillwater Tragedy"*
as a traditional bound book at:
www.1stWorldLibrary.org/purchase.asp?ISBN=1-4218-0495-6

1st World Library Literary Society is a nonprofit
organization dedicated to promoting literacy by:

- Creating a free internet library accessible from any
computer worldwide.
- Hosting writing competitions and offering book
publishing scholarships.

The Stillwater Tragedy
contributed by Tim, Ed & Rodney
in support of
1st World Library Literary Society

I

It is close upon daybreak. The great wall of pines and hemlocks that keep off the west wind from Stillwater stretches black and indeterminate against the sky. At intervals a dull, metallic sound, like the guttural twang of a violin string, rises form the frog-invested swamp skirting the highway. Suddenly the birds stir in their nests over there in the woodland, and break into that wild jargoning chorus with which they herald the advent of a new day. In the apple-orchards and among the plum-trees of the few gardens in Stillwater, the wrens and the robins and the blue-jays catch up the crystal crescendo, and what a melodious racket they make of it with their fifes and flutes and flageolets!

The village lies in a trance like death. Possibly not a soul hears this music, unless it is the watchers at the bedside of Mr. Leonard Tappleton, the richest man in town, who has lain dying these three days, and cannot last until sunrise. Or perhaps some mother, drowsily hushing her wakeful baby, pauses a moment and listens vacantly to the birds singing. But who else?

The hubbub suddenly ceases, - ceases as suddenly as it began, - and all is still again in the woodland. But it is not so dark as before. A faint glow of white light is discernible behind the ragged line of the tree-tops. The deluge of the darkness is receding from the face of the earth, as the mighty waters receded of old.

The roofs and tall factory chimneys of Stillwater are slowly taking shape in the gloom. Is that a cemetery coming into view yonder, with its ghostly architecture of obelisks and broken columns and huddled head-stones? No, that is only Slocum's Marble Yard, with the finished and unfinished work heaped up like snowdrifts, - a cemetery in embryo. Here and there in an outlying farm a lantern glimmers in the barn-yard: the cattle are having their fodder betimes. Scarlet-capped chanticleer gets himself on the nearest rail-fence and lifts up his rancorous voice like some irate old cardinal launching the curse of Rome. Something crawls swiftly along the gray of the serpentine turn-pike, - a cart, with the driver lashing a jaded horse. A quick wind goes shivering by, and is lost in the forest.

Now a narrow strip of two-colored gold stretches along the horizon.

Stillwater is gradually coming to its senses. The sun has begun to twinkle on the gilt cross of the Catholic chapel and make itself known to the doves in the stone belfry of the South Church. The patches of cobweb that here and there cling tremulously to the coarse grass of the inundated meadows have turned into silver nets, and the mill-pond - it will be steel-blue later - is as smooth and white as if it had been paved with one vast unbroken slab out of Slocum's Marble Yard. Through a row of button-woods on the northern skirt of the village is seen a square, lap-streaked building, painted a disagreeable brown, and surrounded on three sides by a platform, - one of seven or eight similar stations strung like Indian heads on a branch thread of the Great Sagamore Railway.

Listen! That is the jingle of the bells on the baker's cart as it begins its rounds. From innumerable chimneys the curdled smoke gives evidence that the thrifty house-wife - or, what is rarer in Stillwater, the hired girl - has lighted the kitchen fire.

The chimney-stack of one house at the end of a small court - the last house on the easterly edge of the village, and standing quite alone - sends up no smoke. Yet the carefully trained ivy over the porch, and the lemon verbena in a tub at the foot of the steps, intimate that the place is not unoccupied. Moreover, the little schooner which acts as weather-cock on one of the gables, and is now heading due west, has a new top-sail. It is a story-and-a-half cottage, with a large expanse of roof, which, covered with porous, unpain-ted shingles, seems to repel the sunshine that now strikes full upon it. The upper and lower blinds on the main building, as well as those on the extensions, are tightly closed. The sun appears to beat in vain at the casement sof this silent house, which has a curiously sullen and defiant air, as if it had desperately and successfully barricaded itself against the approach of morning; yet if one were standing in the room that leads from the bed-chamber on the ground-floor - the room with the latticed window - one would see a ray of light thrust through a chink of the shutters, and pointing like a human finger at an object which lies by the hearth.

This finger, gleaming, motionless, and awful in its precision, points to the body of old Mr. Lemuel Shackford, who lies there dead in his night-dress, with a gash across his forehead.

In the darkness of that summer night a deed darker than the night itself had been done in Stillwater.

Thomas Bailey Aldrich

II

That morning, when Michael Hennessey's girl Mary - a girl sixteen years old - carried the can of milk to the rear door of the silent house, she was nearly a quarter of hour later than usual, and looked forward to being soundly rated.

"He's up and been waiting for it," she said to herself, observing the scullery door ajar. "Won't I ketch it! It's him for growling and snapping at a body, and it's me for always being before or behind time, bad luck to me. There's no plazing him."

Mary pushed back the door and passed through the kitchen, serving herself all the while to meet the objurgations which she supposed were lying in wait for her. The sunshine was blinding without, but sifted through the green jalousies, it made a gray, crepuscular light within. As the girl approached the table, on which a plate with knife and fork had been laid for breakfast, she noticed, somewhat indistinctly at first, a thin red line running obliquely across the floor from the direction of the sitting-room and ending near the stove, where it had formed a small pool. Mary stopped short, scarcely conscious why, and peered instinctively into the adjoining apartment. Then, with a smothered cry, she let fall the milk-can, and a dozen white rivulets, in strange contrast to that one dark red line which first startled her, went meandering over the kitchen floor. With her eyes riveted upon some object in the next room, the girl retreated backward slowly and heavily dragging one foot after the other, until she reached the gallery door; then she turned swiftly, and plunged into the street.

Twenty minutes later, every man, woman, and child in Stillwater knew that old Mr. Shackford had been murdered.

Mary Hennessey had to tell her story a hundred times during the morning, for each minute brought to Michael's tenement a fresh listener hungry for the details at first hand.

"How was it, Molly? Tell a body, dear!"

"Don't be asking me!" cried Molly, pressing her palms to her eyes as if to shut out the sight, but taking all the while a secret creepy satisfaction in living the scene over again. "It was kinder dark in the other room, and there he was, laying in his night-gownd, with his face turned towards me, so, looking mighty severe-like, jest as if he was a-going to say, 'It's late with the milk ye are, ye hussy!' - a way he had of spaking."

"But he didn't spake, Molly darlin'?"

"Niver a word. He was stone dead, don't you see. It was that still you could hear me heart beat, saving there wasn't a drop of beat in it. I let go the can, sure, and then I backed out, with me eye on 'im all the while, afeard to death that he would up and spake them words."

"The pore child! for the likes of her to be wakin' up a murthered man in the mornin'!"

There was little or no work done that day in Stillwater outside the mills, and they were not running full handed. A number of men from the Miantowona Iron Works and Slocum's Yard - Slocum employed some seventy or eighty hands - lounged about the streets in their blouses, or stood in knots in front of the tavern, smoking short clay pipes. Not an urchin put in an appearance at the small red brick building on the turnpike. Mr. Pinkham, the school-master, waited an hour for the recusants, then turned the key in the lock and went home.

Dragged-looking women, with dishcloth or dustpan in hand, stood in door-ways or leaned from windows, talking in subdued voices with neighbors on the curb-stone. In a hundred far-away cities the news of the suburban tragedy had already been read and forgotten; but here the horror stayed.

There was a constantly changing crowd gathered in front of the house in Welch's Court. An inquest was being held in the room adjoining the kitchen. The court, which ended at the gate of the cottage, was fringed for several yards on each side by rows of squalid, wondering children, who understood it that Coroner Whidden was literally to sit on the dead body, - Mr. Whidden, a limp, inoffensive little man, who would not have dared to sit down on a fly. He had passed, pallid and perspiring, to the scene of his perfunctory duties.

The result of the investigation was awaited with feverish impatience by the people outside. Mr.

Shackford had not been a popular man; he had been a hard, avaricious, passionate man, holding his own way remorselessly. He had been the reverse of popular, but he had long been a prominent character in Stillwater, because of his wealth, his endless lawsuits, and his eccentricity, an illustration of which was his persistence in living entirely alone in the isolated and dreary old house, that was henceforth to be inhabited by his shadow. Not his shadow alone, however, for it was now remembered that the premises were already held in fee by another phantasmal tenant. At a period long anterior to this, one Lydia Sloper, a widow, had died an unexplained death under that same roof. The coincidence struck deeply into the imaginative portion of Stillwater. "The Widow Sloper and old Shackford have made a match of it," remarked a local humorist, in a grimmer vain than customary. Two ghosts had now set up housekeeping, as it were, in the stricken mansion, and what might not be looked for in the way of spectral progeny!

It appeared to the crowd in the lane that the jury were unconscionably long in arriving at a decision, and when the decision was at length reached it gave but moderate satisfaction. After a spendthrift waste of judicial mind the jury had decided that "the death of Lemuel Shackford was caused by a blow on the left temple, inflicted with some instrument not discoverable, in the hands of some person or persons unknown."

"We knew that before," grumbled a voice in the crowd, when, to relieve public suspense, Lawyer Perkins - a long, lank man, with stringy black hair - announced the verdict from the doorstep.

The theory of suicide had obtained momentary credence early in the morning, and one or two still clung to it with the tenacity that characterizes persons who entertain few ideas. To accept this theory it was necessary to believe that Mr. Shackford had ingeniously hidden the weapon after striking himself dead with a single blow. No, it was not suicide. So far from intending to take his own life, Mr. Shackford, it appeared, had made rather careful preparations to live that day. The breakfast-table had been laid over night, the coals left ready for kindling in the Franklin stove, and a kettle, filled with water to be heated for his tea or coffee, stood on the hearth.

Two facts had sharply demonstrated themselves: first, that Mr. Shackford had been murdered; and, second, that the spur to the crime had been the possession of a sum of money, which the deceased was supposed to keep in a strong-box in his bedroom. The padlock had been wrenched open, and the less valuable contents of the chest, chiefly papers, scattered over the carpet. A memorandum among the papers seemed to specify the respective sums in notes and gold that had been deposited in the box. A document of some kind had been torn into minute pieces and thrown into the waste-basket. On close scrutiny a word or two here and there revealed the fact that the document was of a legal character. The fragments were put into an envelope and given in charge of Mr. Shackford's lawyer, who placed seals on that and on the drawers of an escritoire which stood in the corner and contained other manuscript.

The instrument with which the fatal blow had been dealt - for the autopsy showed that there had been but one blow - was not only not discoverable, but the fashion of it defied conjecture. The shape of the wound did not indicate the use of any implement known to the jurors, several of whom were skilled machinists. The wound was an inch and three quarters in length and very deep at the extremities; in the middle in scarcely penetrated to the cranium. So peculiar a cut could not have been produced with the claw part of a hammer, because the claw is always curved, and the incision was straight. A flat claw, such as is used in opening packing-cases, was suggested. A collection of the several sizes manufactured was procured, but none corresponded with the wound; they were either too wide or too narrow. Moreover, the cut was as thin as the blade of a case-knife.

"That was never done by any tool in these parts," declared Stevens, the foreman of the finishing shop at Slocum's.

The assassin or assassins had entered by the scullery door, the simple fastening of which, a hook and staple, had been broken. There were footprints in the soft clay path leading from the side gate to the stone step; but Mary Hennessey had so confused and obliterated the outlines that now it was impossible accurately to measure them. A half-burned match was found under the sink, - evidently thrown there by the burglars. It was of a kind known as the safety-match, which can be ignited only by friction on a strip of chemically prepared paper glued to the box. As no box of this description was discovered, and as all the other matches in the house were of a different make, the charred splinter was preserved. The most minute examination failed to show more than this. The last time Mr. Shackford had been seen alive was at six o'clock the previous evening.

Who had done the deed?

Tramps! answered Stillwater, with one voice, though Stillwater lay somewhat out of the natural highway, and the tramp - that bitter blossom of civilization whose seed was blown to us from over seas - was not then so common by the New England roadsides as he became five or six years later. But it was intolerable not to have a theory; it was that or none, for conjecture turned to no one in the village. To be sure, Mr. Shackford had been in litigation with several of the corporations, and had had legal quarrels with more than one of his neighbors; but Mr. Shackford had never been victorious in any of these contests, and the incentive of revenge was wanting to explain the crime. Besides, it was so clearly robbery.

Though the gathering around the Shackford house had reduced itself to half a dozen idlers, and the less frequented streets had resumed their normal aspect of dullness, there was a strange, electric quality in the atmosphere. The community was in that state of suppressed agitation and suspicion which no word adequately describes. The slightest circumstance would have swayed it to the belief in any man's guilt; and, indeed, there were men in Stillwater quite capable of disposing of a fellow-creature for a much smaller reward than Mr. Shackford had held out. In spite of the tramp theory, a harmless tin-peddler, who had not passed through the place for weeks, was dragged from his glittering cart that afternoon, as he drove smilingly into town, and would have been roughly handled if Mr. Richard Shackford, a cousin of the deceased, had not interfered.

As the day wore on , the excitement deepened in

intensity, though the expression of it became nearly reticent. It was noticed that the lamps throughout the village were lighted an hour earlier than usual. A sense of insecurity settled upon Stillwater with the falling twilight, - that nameless apprehension which is possibly more trying to the nerves than tangible danger. When a man is smitten inexplicably, as if by a bodiless hand stretched out of a cloud, - when the red slayer vanishes like a mist and leaves no faintest trace of his identity, - the mystery shrouding the deed presently becomes more appalling than the deed itself. There is something paralyzing in the thought of an invisible hand somewhere ready to strike at your life, or at some life dearer than your own. Whose hand, and where is it? Perhaps it passes you your coffee at breakfast; perhaps you have hired it to shovel the snow off your sidewalk; perhaps it has brushed against you in the crowd; or may be you have dropped a coin into the fearful palm at a street corner. Ah, the terrible unseen hand that stabs your imagination, - this immortal part of you which is a hundred times more sensitive than your poor perishable body!

In the midst of situations the most solemn and tragic there often falls a light purely farcical in its incongruity. Such a gleam was unconsciously projected upon the present crisis by Mr. Bodge, better known in the village as Father Bodge. Mr. Bodge was stone deaf, naturally stupid, and had been nearly moribund for thirty years with asthma. Just before night-fall he had crawled, in his bewildered, wheezy fashion, down to the tavern, where he found a somber crowd in the bar-room. Mr. Bodge ordered his mug of beer, and sat sipping it, glancing meditatively from time to time over the pewter rim at the mute assembly. Suddenly he broke out: "S'pose you've heerd that old Shackford's ben murdered."

So the sun went down on Stillwater. Again the great wall of pines and hemlocks made a gloom against the sky. The moon rose from behind the tree-tops, frosting their ragged edges, and then sweeping up to the zenith hung serenely above the world, as if there were never a crime, or a tear, or a heart-break in it all.

III

On the afternoon of the following day Mr. Shackford was duly buried. The funeral, under the direction of Mr. Richard Shackford, who acted as chief mourner and was sole mourner by right of kinship, took place in profound silence. The carpenters, who had lost a day on Bishop's new stables, intermitted their sawing and hammering while the services were in progress; the steam was shut off in the iron-mills, and no clinking of the chisel was heard in the marble yard for an hour, during which many of the shops had their shutters up. Then, when all was over, the imprisoned fiend in the boilers gave a piercing shriek; the leather bands slipped on the revolving drums, the spindles leaped into life again, and the old order of things was reinstated, - outwardly, but not in effect.

In general, when the grave closes over a man his career is ended. But Mr. Shackford was never so much alive as after they had buried him. Never before had he filled so large a place in the public eye. Though invisible, he sat at every fireside. Until the manner of his death had been made clear, his ubiquitous presence was not to be exorcised. On the morning of the memorable day a reward of one hundred dollars - afterwards increased to five hundred, at the insistence of Mr. Shackford's cousin - had been offered by the board of selectmen for the arrest and conviction of the guilty party. Beyond this and the unsatisfactory inquest, the authorities had done nothing, and were plainly not equal to the situation.

When it was stated, the night of the funeral, that a professional person was coming to Stillwater to look into the case, the announcement was received with a breath of relief.

The person thus vaguely described appeared on the spot the next morning. To mention the name of Edward Taggett is to mention a name well known to the detective force of the great city lying sixty miles southwest of Stillwater. Mr. Taggett's arrival sent such a thrill of expectancy through the village that Mr. Leonard Tappleton, whose obsequies occurred this day, made his exit nearly unobserved. Yet there was little in Mr. Taggett's physical aspect calculated to stir either expectation or enthusiasm: a slender man of about twenty-six, but not looking it, with overhanging brown mustache, sparse side-whiskers, eyes of no definite color, and faintly accentuated eyebrows. He spoke precisely, and with a certain unembarrassed hesitation, as persons do who have two thoughts to one word, - if there are such persons. You might have taken him for a physician, or a journalist, or the secretary of an insurance company; but you would never have supposed him the man who had disen-tangled the complicated threads of the great Barnabee Bank defalcation.

Stillwater's confidence, which had risen into the nineties, fell to zero at sight of him. "Is *that* Taggett?" they asked. That was Taggett; and presently his influence began to be felt like a sea-turn. The three Dogberrys of the watch were dispatched on secret missions, and within an hour it was ferreted out that a man in a cart had been seen driving furiously up the turnpike the morning after the murder. This was an agricultural district, the road led to a market town, and teams going by in the early dawn were the rule and not the exception; but on that especial morning a furiously driven cart was significant. Jonathan Beers, who farmed the Jenks land, had heard the wheels and caught an indistinct glimpse of the vehicle as he was feeding the cattle, but with a reticence purely rustic had not been moved to mention the circumstance before.

"Taggett has got a clew," said Stillwater under its breath.

By noon Taggett had got the man, cart and all. But it was only Blufton's son Tom, of South Millville, who had started in hot haste that particular morning to secure medical service for his wife, of which she had sorely stood in need, as two tiny girls in a willow cradle in South Millville now bore testimony.

"I haven't been cutting down the population *much,*" said Blufton, with his wholesome laugh.

Thomas Blufton was well known and esteemed in Stillwater, but if the crime had fastened itself upon him it would have given something like popular satisfaction.

In the course of the ensuing forty-eight hours four or five tramps were overhauled as having been in the neighborhood at the time of the tragedy; but they each had a clean story, and were let go. Then one Durgin, a workman at Slocum's Yard, was called upon to explain some half-washed-out red stains on his overalls, which he did. He had tightened the hoops on a salt-pork barrel for Mr. Shackford several days previous; the red paint on the head of the barrel was fresh, and had come off on his clothes. Dr. Weld examined the spots under a microscope, and pronounced them paint. It was manifest that Mr. Taggett meant to go to the bottom of things.

The bar-room of the Stillwater hotel was a center of interest these nights; not only the bar-room proper, but the adjoining apartment, where the more exclusive guests took their seltzer-water and looked over the metropolitan newspapers. Twice a week a social club met here, having among its members Mr. Craggie, the postmaster, who was supposed to have a great political future, Mr. Pinkham, Lawyer Perkins, Mr. Whidden, and other respectable persons. The room was at all times in some sense private, with a separate entrance from the street, though another door, which usually stood open, connected it with the main salon. In this was a long mahogany counter, one section of which was covered with a sheet of zinc perforated like a sieve, and kept constantly bright by restless caravans of lager-beer glasses. Directly behind that end of the counter stood a Gothic brass-mounted beer-pump, at whose faucets Mr. Snelling, the landlord, flooded you five or six mugs in the twinkling of an eye, and raised the vague expectation that he was about to grind out some popular operatic air. At the left of the pump stretched a narrow mirror, reflecting he gaily-colored wine-glasses and decanters which stood on each other's shoulders, and held up lemons, and performed various acrobatic feats on a shelf in front of it.

The fourth night after the funeral of Mr. Shackford, a

dismal southeast storm caused an unusual influx of idlers in both rooms. With the rain splashing against the casements and the wind slamming the blinds, the respective groups sat discussing in a desultory way the only topic which could be discussed at present. There had been a general strike among the workmen a fortnight before; but even that had grown cold as a topic.

"That was hard on Tom Blufton," said Stevens, emptying the ashes out of his long-stemmed clay pipe, and refilling the bowl with cut cavendish from a jar on a shelf over his head.

Michael Hennessey sat down his beer-mug with an air of argumentative disgust, and drew one sleeve across his glistening beard.

"Stevens, you've as many minds as a weather-cock, jist! Didn't ye say yerself it looked mighty black for the lad when he was took?"

"I might have said something of the sort," Stevens admitted reluctantly, after a pause. "His driving round at daybreak with an empty cart did have an ugly look at first."

"Indade, then."

"Not to anybody who knew Tom Blufton," interrupted Samuel Piggott, Blufton's brother-in-law. "The boy hasn't a bad streak in him. It was an outrage. Might as well have suspected Parson Langly or Father O'Meara."

"If this kind of thing goes on," remarked a man in the

corner with a patch over one eye, "both of them reverend gents will be hauled up, I shouldn't wonder."

"That's so, Mr. Peters," responded Durgin. "If my respectability didn't save me, who's safe?"

"Durgin is talking about his respectability! He's joking."

"Look here, Dexter," said Durgin, turning quickly on the speaker, "when I want to joke, I talk about your intelligence."

"What kind of man is Taggett, anyhow?" asked Piggott. "You saw him, Durgin."

"I believe he was at Justice Beemis's office the day Blufton and I was there; but I didn't make him out in the crowd. Shouldn't know him from Adam."

"Stillwater's a healthy place for tramps jest about this time," suggested somebody. "Three on 'em snaked in to-day."

"I think, gentlemen, that Mr. Taggett is on the right track there," observed Mr. Snelling, in the act of mixing another Old Holland for Mr. Peters. "Not too sweet, you said? I feel it in my bones that it was a tramp, and that Mr. Taggett will bring him yet."

"He won't find him on the highway yonder," said a tgall, swarthy man named Torrini, an Italian. Nationalities clash in Stillwater. "That tramp is a thousand miles from here."

"So he is if he has any brains under his hat," returned

Snelling. "But they're on the lookout for him. The minute he pawns anything, he's gone."

"Can't put up greenbacks or gold, can he? He didn't take nothing else," interposed Bishop, the veterinary surgeon.

"Now jewelry nor nothing?"

"There wasn't none, as I understand it," said Bishop, "except a silver watch. That was all snug under the old man's piller."

"Wanter know!" ejaculated Jonathan Beers.

"I opine, Mr. Craggie," said the school-master, standing in the inner room with a rolled-up file of the Daily Advertiser in his hand, "that the person who - who removed our worthy townsman will never be discovered."

"I shouldn't like to go quite so far as that, sir," answered Mr. Craggie, with that diplomatic suavity which leads to postmasterships and seats in the General Court, and has even been known to oil a dull fellow's way into Congress. "I cannot take quite so hopeless a view of it. There are difficulties, but they must be overcome, Mr. Pinkham, and I think they will be."

"Indeed, I hope so," returned the school-master. "But there are cases - are there not? - in which the - the problem, if I may so designate it, has never been elucidated, and the persons who undertook it have been obliged to go to the foot, so to speak."

"Ah, yes, there are such cases, certainly. There was the Burdell mystery in New York, and, later, the Nathan affair - By the way, I've satisfactory theories of my own touching both. The police were baffled, and remain so. But, my *dear* sir, observe for a moment the difference."

Mr. Pinkham rested one finger on the edge of a little round table, and leaned forward in a respectful attitude to observe the difference.

"Those crimes were committed in a vast metropolis affording a thousand chances for escape, as well as offering a thousand temptations to the lawless. But we are a limited community. We have no professional murderers among us. The deed which has stirred society to its utmost depths was plainly done by some wayfaring amateur. Remorse has already arrived upon him, if the police haven't. For the time being he escapes; but he is bound to betray himself sooner or later. If the right steps are taken, - and I have myself the greatest confidence in Mr. Taggett, - the guilty party can scarcely fail to be brought to the bar of justice, if he doesn't bring himself there."

"Indeed, indeed, I hope so," repeated Mr. Pinkham.

"The investigation is being carried on very closely."

"Too closely," suggested the school-master.

"Oh dear, no," murmured Mr. Craggie. "The strictest secrecy is necessary in affairs of this delicate nature. If Tom, Dick, and Harry were taken behind the scenes," he added, with the air of one wishing to say too much, "the bottom would drop out of everything."

Mr. Pinkham shrunk from commenting on a disaster like that, and relapsed into silence. Mr. Craggie, with his thumbs in the arm-holes of his waistcoat, and his legs crossed in an easy, senatorial fashion, leaned back in the chair and smiled blandly.

"I don't suppose there's nothing new, boys!" exclaimed a fat, florid man, bustling in good-naturedly at the public entrance, and leaving a straight wet trail on the sanded floor from the threshold to the polished mahogany counter. Mr. Wilson was a local humorist of the Falstaffian stripe, though not so much witty in himself as the cause of wit in others.

"No, Jimmy, there isn't anything new," responded Dexter.

"I suppose you didn't hear that the ole man done somethin' handsome for me in his last will and testyment."

"No, Jemmy, I don't think he has made any provision whatever for an almshouse."

"Sorry to hear that, Dexter," said Willson, absorbedly chasing a bit of lemon peel in his glass with the spoon handle, "for there isn't room for us all up at the town-farm. How's your grandmother? Finds it tol'rably comfortable?"

They are a primitive, candid people in their hours of unlaced social intercourse in Stillwater. This delicate *tu quoque* was so far from wounding Dexter that he replied carelessly, -

"Well, only so so. The old woman complains of too

much chicken-sallid, and hot-house grapes all the year round."

"Mr. Shackford must have left a large property," observed Mr. Ward, of the firm of Ward & Lock, glancing up from the columns of the Stillwater Gazette. The remark was addressed to Lawyer Perkins, who had just joined the group in the reading-room.

"Fairly large," replied that gentleman crisply.

"Any public bequests?"

"None to speak of."

Mr. Craggie smiled vaguely.

"You see," said Lawyer Perkins, "there's a will and no will, - that is to say, the fragments of what is supposed to be a will were found, and we are trying to put the pieces together. It is doubtful if we can do it; it is doubtful if we can decipher it after we have done it; and if we decipher it it is a question whether the document is valid or not."

"That is a masterly exposition of the dilemma, Mr. Perkins," said the school-master warmly.

Mr. Perkins had spoken in his court-room tone of voice, with one hand thrust into his frilled shirt-bosom. He removed this hand for a second, as he gravely bowed to Mr. Pinkham.

"Nothing could be clearer," said Mr. Ward. "In case the paper is worthless, what then? I am not asking you in your professional capacity," he added hastily; for

Lawyer Perkins had been known to send in a bill on as slight a provocation as Mr. Ward's.

"That's a point. The next of kin has his claims."

"My friend Shackford, of course," broke in Mr. Craggie. "Admirable young man! - one of my warmest supporters."

"He is the only heir at law so far as we know," said Mr. Perkins.

"Oh," said Mr. Craggie, reflecting. "The late Mr. Shackford might have had a family in Timbuctoo or the Sandwich Islands."

"That's another point."

"The fact would be a deuced unpleasant point for young Shackford to run against," said Mr. Ward.

"Exactly."

"If Mr. Lemuel Shackford," remarked Coroner Whidden, softly joining the conversation to which he had been listening in his timorous, apologetic manner, "had chanced, in the course of his early sea-faring days, to form any ties of an unhappy complexion" -

"Complexion is good," murmured Mr. Craggie. "Some Hawaiian lady!"

- "perhaps that would be a branch of the case worth investigating in connection with the homicide. A discarded wife, or a disowned son, burning with a sense of wrong" -

"Really, Mr. Whidden!" interrupted Lawyer Perkins witheringly, "it is bad enough for my client to lose his life, without having his reputation filched away from him."

"I - I will explain! I was merely supposing" -

"The law never supposes, sir!"

This threw Mr. Whidden into great mental confusion. As coroner was he not an integral part of the law, and when, in his official character, he supposed anything was not that a legal supposition? But was he in his official character now, sitting with a glass of lemonade at his elbow in the reading-room of the Stillwater hotel? Was he, or was he not, a coroner all the time? Mr. Whidden stroked an isolated tuft of hair growing low on the middle of his forehead, and glared mildly at Mr. Perkins.

"Young Shackford has gone to New York, I understand," said Mr. Ward, breaking the silence.

Mr. Perkins nodded. "Went this morning to look after the real-estate interests there. It will probably keep him a couple of weeks, - the longer the better. He was of no use here. Lemuel's death was a great shock to him, or rather the manner of it was."

"That shocked every one. They were first cousin's weren't they?" Mr. Ward was a comparatively new resident in Stillwater.

"First cousins," replied Lawyer Perkins; "but they were never very intimate, you know."

"I imagine nobody was ever very intimate with Mr. Shackford."

"My client was somewhat peculiar in his friendships."

This was stating it charitably, for Mr. Perkins knew, and every one present knew, that Lemuel Shackford had not had the shadow of a friend in Stillwater, unless it was his cousin Richard.

A cloud of mist and rain was blown into the bar-room as the street door stood open for a second to admit a dripping figure from the outside darkness.

"What's blowed down?" asked Durgin, turning round on his stool and sending up a ring of smoke which uncurled itself with difficulty in the dense atmosphere.

"It's only some of Jeff Stavers's nonsense."

"No nonsense at all," said the new-comer, as he shook the heavy beads of rain from his felt hat. "I was passing by Welch's Court - it's as black as pitch out, fellows - when slap went something against my shoulder; something like wet wings. Well, I was scared. It's a bat, says I. But the thing didn't fly off; it was still clawing at my shoulder. I put up my hand, and I'll be shot if it wasn't the foremast, jib-sheet and all, of the old weather-cock on the north gable of the Shackford house! Here you are!" and the speaker tossed the broken mast, with the mimic sails dangling from it, into Durgin's lap.

A dead silence followed, for there wa felt to be something weirdly significant in the incident.

"That's kinder omernous," said Mr. Peters, interrogatively.

"Ominous of what?" asked Durgin, lifting the wet mass from his knees and dropping it on the floor.

"Well, sorter queer, then."

"Where does the queer come in?" inquired Stevens, gravely. "I don't know; but I'm hit by it."

"Come, boys, don't crowd a feller," said Mr. Peters, getting restive. "I don't take the contract to explain the thing. But it does seem some way droll that the old schooner should be wrecked so soon after what has happened to the old skipper. If you don't see it, or sense it, I don't insist. What's yours, Denyven?"

The person addressed as Denyven promptly replied, with a fine sonorous English accent, "a mug of 'alf an' 'alf, - with a head on it, Snelling."

At the same moment Mr. Craggie, in the inner room was saying to the school-master, -

"I must really take issue with you there, Mr. Pinkham. I admit there's a good deal in spiritualism which we haven't got at yet; the science is in its infancy; it is still attached to the bosom of speculation. It is a beautiful science, that of psychological phenomena, and the spiritualists will yet become an influential class of" - Mr. Craggie was going to say voters, but glided over it - "persons. I believe in clairvoyance myself to a large extent. Before my appointment to the post-office I had it very strong. I've no doubt that in the far future this mysterious factor will be made great use of in criminal cases; but at present I should resort to it only in the last extremity, - the very last extremity, Mr. Pinkham!"

"Oh, of course," said the school-master deprecatingly. "I threw it out only as the merest suggestion. I shouldn't think of - of - you understand me?"

"Is it beyond the dreams of probability," said Mr. Craggie, appealing to Lawyer Perkins, "that clairvoyants may eventually be introduced into cases in our courts?"

"They are now," said Mr. Perkins, with a snort, - "the police bring 'em it."

Mr. Craggie finished the remainder of his glass of sherry in silence, and presently rose to go. Coroner Whidden and Mr. Ward had already gone. The guests in the public room were thinning out; a gloom, indefinable and shapeless like the night, seemed to have fallen upon the few that lingered. At a somewhat earlier hour tdhan usual the gas was shut off in the Stillwater hotel.

In the lonely house in Welch's Court a light was still burning.

IV

A sorely perplexed man sat there, bending over his papers by the lamp-light. Mr. Taggett had established himself at the Shackford house on his arrival, preferring it to the hotel, where he would have been subjected to the curiosity of the guests and to endless annoyances. Up to this moment, perhaps not a dozen persons in the place had had more than a passing glimpse of him. He was a very busy man, working at his desk from morning until night, and then taking only a brief walk, for exercise in some unfrequented street. His meals were sent in from the hotel to the Shackford house, where the constables reported to him, and where he held protracted conferences with Justice Beemis, Coroner Whidden, Lawyer Perkins, and a few others, and declined to be interviewed by the local editor.

To the outside eye that weather-stained, faded old house appeared a throbbing seat of esoteric intelligence. It was as if a hundred invisible magnetic threads converged to a focus under that roof and incessantly clicked ouit the most startling information, - information which was never by any chance allowed to pass beyond the charmed circle. The pile of letters which the mail brought to Mr. Taggett every morning - chiefly anonymous suggestions, and offers of assistance from lunatics in remote cities - was enough in itself to expasperate a community.

Covertly at first, and then openly, Stillwater began seriously to question Mr. Taggett's method of working up the case. The Gazette, in a double-leaded leader, went so far as to compare him to a bird with fine feathers and no song, and to suggest that perhaps the bird might have sung if the inducement offered had been more substantial. A singer of Mr. Taggett's plumage was not to be taught by such chaff as five hundred dollars. Having killed his man, the editor proceeded to remark that he would suspend judgment until next week.

As if to make perfect the bird comparison, Mr. Taggett, after keeping the public in suspense for six days and nights, abruptly flew away, with all the little shreds and straws of evidence he had picked up, to build his speculative nest elsewhere.

The defection of Mr. Taggett caused a mild panic among a certain portion of the inhabitants, who were not reassured by the statement in the Gazette that the case would now be placed in the proper hands, - the hand so the county constabulary. "Within a few days," said the editor in conclusion, "the matter will undoubtedly be cleared up. At present we cannot say more;" and it would have puzzled him very much to do so.

A week passed, and no fresh light was thrown upon the catastrophe, nor did anything occur to rattle the usual surface of life in the village. A man - it was Torrini, the Italian - got hurt in Dana's iron foundry; one of Blufton's twin girls died; and Mr. Slocum took on a new hand from out of town. That was all. Stillwater was the Stillwater of a year ago, with always the exception of that shadow lying upon it, and the fact that small boys who had kindling to get in were careful to get it in before nightfall. It would appear that the late Mr. Shackford had acquired a habit of lingering around wood-plies after dark, and also of stealing into bed-chambers, where little children were obliged to draw the sheets over their heads in order not to see him.

The action of the county constabulary had proved quite as mysterious and quite as barren of result as Mr. Taggett's had been. They had worn his mantle of secrecy, and arrested the tramps over again.

Another week dragged by, and the editorial prediction seemed as far as ever from fulfillment. But on the afternoon which closed that fortnight a very singular thing did happen. Mr. Slocum was sitting alone in his office, which occupied the whole of a small building at the right of the main gate to the marble works. When the door behind him softly opened and a young man, whose dress covered with stone-dust indicated his vocation, appeared on the threshold. He hesitated a second, and then stepped into the room. Mr. Slocum turned round with a swift, apprehensive air.

"You gave me a start! I believe I haven't any nerves left. Well?"

"Mr. Slocum, I have found the man."

The proprietor of the marble yard half rose from the desk in his agitation.

"Who is it?" he asked beneath his breath.

The same doubt or irresolution which had checked the workman at the threshold seemed again to have taken possession of him. It was fully a moment before he gained the mastery over himself; but the mastery was complete; for he leaned forward gravely, almost coldly, and pronounced two words. A quick pallor overspread Mr. Slocum's features.

"Good God!" he exclaimed, sinking back into the chair. "Are you mad?"

V

The humblest painter of real life, if he could have his desire, would select a picturesque background for his figures; but events have an inexorable fashion for choosing their own landscape. In the present instance it is reluctantly conceded that there are few uglier or more commonplace towns in New England than Stillwater, - a straggling, overgrown village, with whose rural aspects are curiously blended something of the grimness and squalor of certain shabby city neighborhoods. Being of comparatively recent date, the place has none of those colonial associations which, like sprigs of lavender in an old chest of drawers, are a saving grace to other quite as dreary nooks and corners.

Here and there at what is termed the West End is a neat brick mansion with garden attached, where nature asserts herself in dahlias and china-asters; but the houses are mostly frame houses that have taken a prevailing dingy tint from the breath of the tall chimneys which dominate the village. The sidewalks in the more aristocratic quarter are covered with a thin, elastic paste of asphalte, worn down to the gravel in patches, and emitting in the heat of the day an astringent, bituminous odor. The population is chiefly of the rougher sort, such as breeds in the shadow of foundries and factories, and if the Protestant pastor and the fatherly Catholic priest, whose respective lots are cast there, have sometimes the sense of being missionaries dropped in the midst of a purely savage community, the delusion is not wholly unreasonable.

The irregular heaps of scoria that have accumulated in the vicinity of the iron works give the place an illusive air of antiquity; bit it is neither ancient nor picturesque. The oldest and most pictorial thing in Stillwater is probably the marble yard, around three sides of which the village may be said to have sprouted up rankly, bearing here and there an industrial blossom in the shape of an iron-mill or a cardigan-jacket manufactory. Rowland Slocum, a man of considerable refinement, great kindness of heart, and no force, inherited the yard from his father, and a the period this narrative opens (the summer of 187-) was its sole proprietor and nominal manager, the actual manager being Richard Shackford, a prospective partner in the business and the betrothed of Mr. Slocum's daughter Margaret.

Forty years ago every tenth person in Stillwater was either a Shackford or a Slocum. Twenty years later both names were nearly extinct there. That fatality which seems to attend certain New England families had stripped every leaf but two from the Shackford branch. These were Lemuel Shackford, then about forty-six, and Richard Shackford, aged four. Lemuel Shackford had laid up a competency as ship-master in the New York and Calcutta trade, and in 1852 had returned to his native village, where he found his name and stock represented only by little Dick, a very cheerful orphan, who stared complacently with big blue eyes at fate, and made mud-pies in the lane whenever he could elude the vigilance of the kindly old woman who had taken him under her roof. This atom of humanity, by some strange miscalculation of nature, was his cousin.

The strict devotion to his personal interests which had enabled Mr. Shackford to acquire a fortune thus early caused him to look askance at a penniless young kinsman with stockings down at heel, and a straw hat three sizes too large for him set on the back of his head. But Mr. Shackford was ashamed to leave little Dick a burden upon the hands of a poor woman of no relationship whatever to the child; so little Dick was transferred to that dejected house which has already been described, and was then known as the Sloper house.

Here, for three of four years, Dick grew up, as neglected as a weed, and every inch as happy. It should be mentioned that for the first year or so a shock-headed Cicely from the town-farm had apparently been hired not to take care of him. But Dick asked nothing better than to be left to his own devices, which, moreover, were innocent enough. He would sit all day in the lane at the front gate pottering with a bit of twig or a case-knife in the soft clay. From time to time passers-by observed that the child was not making mud-pies, but tracing figures, comic or grotesque as might happen, and always quite wonderful for their lack of resemblance to anything human. That patch of reddish-brown clay was his sole resource, his slate, his drawing-book, and woe to anybody who chanced to walk over little Dick's arabesques. Patient and gentle in his acceptance of the world's rebuffs, this he would not endure. He was afraid of Mr. Shackford, yet one day, when the preoccupied man happened to trample on a newly executed hieroglyphic, the child rose to his feet white with rage, his fingers clenched, and such a blue fire flashing in the eyes that Mr. Shackford drew back aghast.

"Why, it's a little devil!"

While Shackford junior was amusing himself with his primitive bas-reliefs, Shackford senior amused himself with his lawsuits. From the hour when he returned to the town until the end of his days Mr. Shackford was up to his neck in legal difficulties. Now he resisted a betterment assessment, and fought the town; now he secured an injunction on the Miantowona Iron Works, and fought the corporation. He was understood to have a perpetual case in equity before the Marine Court in New York, to which city he made frequent and unannounced journeys. His immediate neighbors stood in terror of him. He was like a duelist, on the alert to twist the slightest thing into a *casus belli*. The law was his rapier, his recreation, and he was willing to bleed for it.

Meanwhile that fairy world of which every baby becomes a Columbus so soon as it is able to walk remained an undiscovered continent to little Dick. Grim life looked in upon him as he lay in the cradle. The common joys of childhood were a sealed volume to him. A single incident of those years lights up the whole situation. A vague rumor had been blown to Dick of a practice of hanging up stockings at Christmas. It struck his materialistic mind as a rather senseless thing to do; but nevertheless he resolved to try it one Christmas Eve. He lay awake a long while in the frosty darkness, skeptically waiting for something remarkable to happen; once he crawled out of the cot-bed and groped his way to the chimney place. The next morning he was scarcely disappointed at finding nothing in the piteous little stocking, except the original holes.

The years that stole silently over the heads of the old man and the young child in Welch's Court brought a period of wild prosperity to Stillwater. The breath of war blew the forges to a white heat, and the baffling problem of the mediæval alchemists was solved. The baser metals were transmuted into gold. A disastrous, prosperous time, with the air rent periodically by the cries of newsboys as battles were fought, and by the roll of the drum in the busy streets as fresh recruits were wanted. Glory and death to the Southward, and at the North pale women in black.

All which interested Dick mighty little. After he had learned to read at the district school, he escaped into another world. Two lights were now generally seen burning of a night in the Shackford house: one on the ground-floor where Mr. Shackford sat mouthing his contracts and mortgages, and weaving his webs like a great, lean, gray spider; and the other in the north gable, where Dick hung over a tattered copy of Robinson Crusoe by the flicker of the candle-ends which he had captured during the day.

Little Dick was little Dick no more: a tall, heavily built blond boy, with a quiet, sweet disposition, that at first offered temptations to the despots of the playground; but a sudden flaring up once or twice of that unexpected spirit which had broken out in his babyhood brought him immunity from serious persecution.

The boy's home life at this time would have seemed pathetic to an observer, - the more pathetic, perhaps, in that Dick himself was not aware of its exceptional barrenness. The holidays that bring new brightness to the eyes of happier children were to him simply days when he did not go to school, and was expected to provide an extra quantity of kindling wood. He was housed, and fed, and clothed, after a fashion, but not loved. Mr. Shackford did not ill-treat the lad, in the sense of beating him; he merely neglected him. Every year the man became more absorbed in his law cases and his money, which accumulated magically. He dwelt in a cloud of calculations. Though all his interests attached him to the material world, his dry, attenuated body seemed scarcely a part of it.

"Shackford, what are you going to do with that scapegrace of yours?"

It was Mr. Leonard Tappleton who ventured the question. Few persons dared to interrogate Mr. Shackford on his private affairs.

"I am going to make a lawyer of him," said Mr. Shackford, crackling his finger-joints like stiff parchment.

"You couldn't do better. You *ought* to have an attorney in the family."

"Just so," assented Mr. Shackford, dryly. "I could throw a bit of business in his way now and then, - eh?"

"You could make his fortune, Shackford. I don't see but you might employ him all the time. When he was not fighting the corporations, you might keep him at it suing you for his fees."

"Very good, very good indeed," responded Mr. Shackford, with a smile in which his eyes took no share, it was merely a momentary curling up of crisp wrinkles. He did not usually smile at other people's pleasantries; but when a person worth three or four hundred thousand dollars condescends to indulge a joke, it is not to be passed over like that of a poor relation. "Yes, yes," muttered the old man, as he stooped and picked up a pin, adding it to a row of similarly acquired pins which gave the left lapel of his threadbare coat the appearance of a miniature harp, "I shall make a lawyer of him."

It had long been settled in Mr. Shackford's mind that Richard, so soon as he had finished his studies, should enter the law-office of Blandmann & Sharpe, a firm of rather sinister reputation in South Millville.

At fourteen Richard's eyes had begun to open on the situation; at fifteen he saw very clearly; and one day, without much preliminary formulating of his plan, he decided on a step that had been taken by every male Shackford as far back as tradition preserves the record of his family.

A friendship had sprung up between Richard and one William Durgin, a school-mate. This Durgin was a sallow, brooding boy, a year older than himself. The two lads were antipodal in disposition, intelligence, and social standing; for though Richard went poorly clad, the reflection of his cousin's wealth gilded him. Durgin was the son of a washerwoman. An intimacy between the two would perhaps have been unlikely but for one fact: it was Durgin's mother who had given little Dick a shelter at the period of his parents' death. Though the circumstance did not lie within the pale of

Richard's personal memory, he acknowledged the debt by rather insisting on Durgin's friendship. It was William Durgin, therefore, who was elected to wait upon Mr. Shackford on a certain morning which found that gentleman greatly disturbed by an unprecedented occurrence, - Richard had slept out of the house the previous night.

Durgin was the bearer of a note which Mr. Shackford received in some astonishment, and read deliberately, blinking with weak eyes behind the glasses. Having torn off the blank page and laid it aside for his own more economical correspondence (the rascal had actually used a whole sheet to write ten words!), Mr. Shackford turned, and with the absorbed air of a naturalist studying some abnormal bug gazed over the steel bow of his spectacles at Durgin.

"Skit!"

Durgin hastily retreated.

"There's a poor lawyer saved," muttered the old man, taking down his overcoat from a peg behind the door, and snapping off a shred of lint on the collar with his lean forefinger. Then his face relaxed, and an odd grin diffused a kind of wintry glow over it.

Richard had run away to sea.

VI

After a lapse of four years, during which he had as completely vanished out of the memory of Stillwater as if he had been lying all the while in the crowded family tomb behind the South Church, Richard Shackford reappeared one summer morning at the door of his cousin's house in Welch's Court. Mr. Shackford was absent at the moment, and Mrs. Morganson, an elderly deaf woman, who came in for a few hours every day to do the house-work, was busy in the extension. Without announcing himself, Richard stalked up-stairs to the chamber in the gable, and went directly to a little shelf in one corner, upon which lay the dog's-eared copy of Robinson Crusoe just as he had left it, save the four years' accumulation of dust. Richard took the book fiercely in both hands, and with a single mighty tug tore it from top to bottom, and threw the fragments into the fire-place.

A moment later, on the way down-stairs, he encountered his kinsman ascending.

"Ah, you have come back!" was Mr. Shackford's grim greeting after a moment's hesitation.

"Yes," said Richard, with embarrassment, though he had made up his mind not to be embarrassed by his cousin.

"I can't say I was looking for you. You might have dropped me a line; you were politer when you left. Why do you come back, and why did you go away?" demanded the old man, with abrupt fierceness. The last four years had bleached him and bent him and made him look very old.

"I didn't like the idea of Blandmann & Sharpe, for one thing," said Richard, "and I thought I liked the sea."

"And did you?"

"No, sir! I enjoyed seeing foreign parts, and all that."

"Quite the young gentleman on his travels. But the sea didn't agree with you, and now you like the idea of Blandmann & Sharpe?"

"Not the least in the world, I assure you!" cried Richard. "I take to it as little as ever I did."

"Perhaps that is fortunate. But it's going to be rather difficult to suit your tastes. What *do* you like?"

"I like you, cousin Lemuel; you have always been kind to me - in your way," said poor Richard, yearning for a glimmer of human warmth and sympathy, and forgetting all the dreariness of his uncared-for childhood. He had been out in the world, and had found it even harder-hearted than his own home, which now he idealized in the first flush of returning to it. Again he saw himself, a blond-headed little fellow with stocking down at heel, climbing the steep staircase, or digging in the clay at the front gate with the air full of the breath of lilacs. That same penetrating perfume, blown through the open hall-door as he spoke, nearly brought the tears to his eyes. He had looked forward for years to this coming back to Stillwater. Many a time, as he wandered along the streets of some foreign sea-port, the rich architecture and the bright costumes had faded out before him, and given place to the fat gray belfry and slim red chimneys of the humble New England village where he was born. He had learned to love it after losing it; and now he had struggled back through countless trials and disasters to find no welcome.

"Cousin Lemuel," said Richard gently, "only just us two are left, and we ought to be good friends, at least."

"We are good enough friends," mumbled Mr. Shackford, who cold not evade taking the hand which Richard had forlornly reached out to him, "but that needn't prevent us understanding each other like rational creatures. I don't care for a great deal of fine sentiment in people who run away without so much as thank'e."

"I was all wrong!"

"That's what folks always say, with the delusion that it makes everything all right."

"Surely it help, - to admit it."

"That depends; it generally doesn't. What do you propose to do?"

"I hardly know at the moment; my plans are quite in the air."

" In the air ! " repeated Mr. Shackford. "I fancy that

describes them. Your father's plans were always in the air, too, and he never got any of them down."

"I intend to get mine down."

"Have you saved by anything?"

"Not a cent."

"I thought as much."

"I had a couple of hundred dollars in my sea-chest; but I was shipwrecked, and lost it. I barely saved myself. When Robinson Crusoe" -

"Damn Robinson Crusoe!" snapped Mr. Shackford.

"That's what I say," returned Richard gravely. "When Robinson Crusoe was cast on an uninhabited island, shrimps and soft-shell crabs and all sorts of delicious mollusks - readily boiled, I've no doubt - crawled up on the beach, and begged him to eat them; but *I* nearly starved to death."

"Of course. You will always be shipwrecked, and always be starved to death; you are one of that kind. I don't believe you are a Shackford at all. When they were not anything else they were good sailors. If you only had a drop of *his* blood in your veins!" and Mr. Shackford waved his head towards a faded portrait of a youngish, florid gentleman with banged hair and high coat-collar, which hung against the wall half-way up the stair-case. This was the counterfeit presentment of Lemuel Shackford's father seated with his back at an open window, through which was seen a ship under full canvas with the union-jack standing out straight in

Thomas Bailey Aldrich

the wrong direction. "But what are you going to do for yourself? You can't start a subscription paper, and play with shipwrecked mariner, you know."

"No, I hardly care to do that," said Richard, with a good-natured laugh, "though no poor devil ever had a better outfit for the character."

"What *are* you calculated for?"

Richard was painfully conscious of his unfitness for many things; but he felt there was nothing in life to which he was so ill adapted as his present position. Yet, until he could look about him, he must needs eat his kinsman's reluctant bread, or starve. The world was younger and more unsophisticated when manna dropped fro the clouds.

Mr. Shackford stood with his neck craned over the frayed edge of his satin stock and one hand resting indecisively on the banister, and Richard on the step above, leaning his back against the blighted flowers of the wall-paper. From an oval window at the head of the stairs the summer sunshine streamed upon them, and illuminated the high-shouldered clock which, ensconced in an alcove, seemed top be listening to the conversation.

"There's no chance for you in the law," said Mr. Shackford, after a long pause. "Sharpe's nephew has the berth. A while ago I might have got you into the Miantowona Iron Works; but the rascally directors are trying to ruin me now. There's the Union Store, if they happen to want a clerk. I suppose you would be about as handy behind a counter as a hippopotamus. I have no business of my own to train you to. You are not good for the sea, and the sea has probably spoiled you for anything else. A drop of salt water just poisons a landsman. I am sure I don't know what to do with you."

"Don't bother yourself about it at all," said Richard, cheerfully. "You are going back on the whole family, ancestors and posterity, by suggesting that I can't make my own living. I only want a little time to take breath, don't you see, and a crust and a bed for a few days, such as you might give any wayfarer. Meanwhile, I will look after things around the place. I fancy I was never an idler here since the day I learnt to split kindling."

"There's your old bed in the north chamber," said Mr. Shackford, wrinkling his forehead helplessly. "According to my notion, it is not so good as a bunk, or a hammock slung in a tidy forecastle, but it's at your service, and Mrs. Morganson, I dare say, can lay an extra plate at table."

With which gracious acceptance of Richard's proposition, Mr. Shackford resumed his way upstairs, and the young man thoughtfully descended to the hall-door and thence into the street, to take a general survey of the commercial capabilities of Stillwater.

The outlook was not inspiring. A machinist, or a mechanic, or a day laborer might have found a foot-hold. A man without handicraft was not in request in Stillwater. "What is your trade?" was the staggering question that met Richard at the threshold. He went from workshop to workshop, confidently and cheer-fully at first, whistling softly between whiles; but at every turn the question confronted him. In some places, where he was recognized with thinly veiled surprise as that boy of Shackford's, he was kindly put off; in others he received only a stare or a brutal No.

By noon he had exhausted the leading shops and offices in the village, and was so disheartened that he began to dread the thought of returning home to dinner. Clearly, he was a superfluous person in Still-water. A mortar-splashed hod-carrier, who had seated himself on a pile of brick and was eating his noonday rations from a tin can just brought to him by a slatternly girl, gave Richard a spasm of envy. Here was a man who had found his place, and was establishing - what Richard did not seem able to establish in his own case - a right to exist.

At supper Mr. Shackford refrained from examining Richard on his day's employment, for which reserve, or indifference, the boy was grateful. When the silent meal was over the old man went to his papers, and Richard withdrew to his room in the gable. He had neglected to provide himself with a candle. Howwever, there was nothing to read, for in destroying Robinson Crusoe he had destroyed his entire library; so he sat and brooded in the moonlight, casting a look of disgust now and then at the mutilated volume on the hearth. That lying romance! It had been, indirectly, the cause of all his woe, filling his boyish brain with visions of picturesque adventure, and sending him off to sea, where he had lost four precious years of his life.

"If I had stuck to my studies," reflected Richard while undressing, "I might have made something of myself. He's a great friend, Robinson Crusoe."

Richard fell asleep with as much bitterness in his

bosom against DeFoe's ingenious hero as if Robinson had been a living person instead of a living fiction, and out of this animosity grew a dream so fantastic and comical that Richard awoke himself with a bewildered laugh just as the sunrise reddened the panes of the chamber window. In this dream somebody came to Richard and asked him if he had heard of that dreadful thing about young Crusoe.

"No, confound him!" said Richard, "what is it?"

"It has been ascertained," said somebody, who seemed to Richard at once an intimate friend and an utter stranger, - "it has been ascertained beyond a doubt that the man Friday was not a man Friday at all, but a light-minded young princess from one of the neighboring islands who had fallen in love with Robinson. Her real name was Saturday."

"Why, that's scandalous!" cried Richard with heat. "Think of the admiration and sympathy the world has been lavishing on this precious pair; Robinson Crusoe and his girl Saturday! That puts a different face on it."

"Another great moral character exploded," murmured the shadowy shape, mixing itself up with the motes of a sunbeam and drifting out through the window. Then Richard fell to laughing in his sleep, and so awoke. He was still confused with the dream as he sat on the edge of his bed, pulling himself together in the broad daylight.

"Well," he muttered at length, "I shouldn't wonder! There's nothing too bad to be believed of that man."

VII

Richard made an early start that morning in search of employment, and duplicated the failure of the previous day. Nobody wanted him. If nobody wanted him in the village where he was born and bred, a village of counting-rooms and workshops, was any other place likely to need him? He had only one hope, if it could be called a hope; at any rate, he had treated it tenderly as such and kept it for the last. He would apply to Rowland Slocum. Long ago, when Richard was an urchin making pot-hooks in the lane, the man used occasionally to pat him on the head and give him pennies. This was not a foundation on which to rear a very lofty castle; but this was all he had.

It was noon when Richard approached the marble yard, and the men were pouring out into the street through the wide gate in the rough deal fence which inclosed the works, - heavy, brawny men, covered with fine white dust, who shouldered each other like cattle, and took the sidewalk to themselves. Richard stepped aside to let them pass, eying them curiously as possible comrades. Suddenly a slim dark fellow, who had retained his paper cap and leather apron, halted and thrust forth a horny hand. The others went on.

"Hullo, Dick Shackford!"

"What, is that you, Will? *You* here?"

"Been here two years now. One of Slocum's apprentices," added Durgin, with an air of easy grandeur.

"Two years? How time flies - when it doesn't crawl! Do you like it?"

"My time will be out next - Oh, the work? Well, yes; it's not bad, and there's a jolly set in the yard. But how about you? I heard last night you'd got home. Been everywhere and come back wealthy? The boys used to say you was off pirating."

"No such luck," answered Richard, with a smile. "I didn't prey on the high seas, - quite the contrary. The high sea captured my kit and four years' savings. I will tell you about it some day. If I have a limb to my name and a breath left to my body, it is no thanks to the Indian Ocean. That is all I have got, Will, and I am looking around for bread and butter, - literally bread and butter."

"No? and the old gentleman so rich!"

Durgin said this with sincere indignation, and was perhaps unconscious himself of experiencing that nameless, shadowy satisfaction which Rochefoucauld says we find in the adversity of our best friends. Certainly Richard looked very seedy in his suit of slop-shop clothes.

"I was on my way to Mr. Slocum's to see if I could do anything with him," Richard continued.

"To get a job, do you mean?"

"Yes, to get work, - to learn *how* to work; to master a trade, in short."

"You can't be an apprentice, you know," said Durgin.

"Why not?"

"Slocum has two."

"Suppose he should happen to want another? He might."

"The Association wouldn't allow it."

"What Association?"

"The Marble Workers' Association, of course."

"They wouldn't allow it! How is that?"

"This the way of it. Slocum is free to take on two apprentices every year, but no more. That prevents workmen increasing too fast, and so keeps up wages. The Marble Workers' Association is a very neat thing, I can tell you."

"But doesn't Mr. Slocum own the yard? I thought he did."

"Yes, he owns the yard."

"If he wished to extend the business, couldn't he employ more hands?"

"As many as he could get, - skilled workmen; but not apprentices."

"And Mr. Slocum agrees to that?" inquired Richard.

"He does."

"And likes it?"

"Not he, - he hates it; but he can't help himself."

"Upon my soul, I don't see what prevents him taking on as many apprentices as he wants to."

"Why, the Association, to be sure," returned Durgin, glancing at the town clock, which marked seven minutes past the hour.

"But how could they stop him?"

"In plenty of ways. Suppose Slocum has a lot of unfinished contracts on hand, - he always has fat contracts, - and the men was to knock off work. That would be kind of awkward, wouldn't it?"

"For a day or two, yes. He could send out of town for hands," suggested Richard.

"And they wouldn't come, if the Association said 'Stay where you are.' They are mostly in the ring. Some outsiders might come, though."

"Then what?"

"Why, then the boys would make it pretty hot for them in Stillwater. Don't you notice?"

"I notice there is not much chance for me," said Richard, despondingly. "Isn't that so?"

"Can't say. Better talk with Slocum. But I must get along; I have to be back sharp at one. I want to hear about your knocking around the worst kind. Can't we meet somewhere tonight, - at the tavern?"

"The tavern? That didn't used to be a quiet place."

"It isn't quiet now, but there's nowhere else to go of a night. It's a comfortable den, and there's always some capital fellows dropping in. A glass of lager with a mate is not a bad thing after a hard day's work."

"Both are good things when they are of the right sort."

"That's like saying I'm not the right sort, isn't it?"

"I meant nothing of the kind. But I don't take to the tavern. Not that I'm squeamish; I have lived four years among sailors, and have been in rougher places than you ever dreamed of; but all the same I am afraid of the tavern. I've seen many a brave fellow wrecked on that reef."

"You always was a bit stuck up," said Durgin candidly.

"Not an inch. I never had much reason to be; and less now than ever, when I can scarcely afford to drink water, let alone beer. I will drop round to your mother's some evening - I hope she's well, - and tell you of my ups and downs. That will be pleasanter for all hands."

"Oh, as you like."

"Now for Mr. Slocum, though you have taken the wind out of me."

The two separated, Durgin with a half smile on his lip, and Richard in a melancholy frame of mind. He passed from the grass-fringed street into the deserted marble yard, where it seemed as if the green summer had suddenly turned into white winter, and threading his way between the huge drifts of snowy stone, knocked at the door of Mr. Slocum's private office.

William Durgin had summed up the case fairly enough as it stood between the Marble Workers' Association and Rowland Slocum. The system of this branch of the trades-union kept trained workmen comparatively scarce, and enabled them to command regular and even advanced prices at periods when other trades were depressed. The older hands looked upon a fresh apprentice in the yard with much the same favor as workingmen of the era of Jacquard looked upon the introduction of a new piece of machinery. Unless the apprentice had exceptional tact, he underwent a rough novitiate. In any case he served a term of social ostracism before he was admitted to full comradeship. Mr. Slocum could easily have found openings each year for a dozen learners, had the matter been under his control; but it was not. "I am the master of each man individually," he declared, "but collectively they are my master." So his business, instead of naturally spreading and becoming a benefit to the many, was kept carefully pruned down to the benefit of the few. He was often forced to decline important contracts, the filling of which would have resulted to the advantage of every person in the village.

Mr. Slocum recognized Richard at once, and listened kindly to his story. It was Mr. Slocum's way to listen kindly to every one; but he was impressed with Richard's intelligence and manner, and became desirous, for several reasons, to assist him. In the first place, there was room in the shops for another apprentice; experienced hands were on jobs that could have been as well done by beginners; and, in the second place, Mr. Slocum had an intuition that Lemuel Shackford was not treating the lad fairly, though Richard had said nothing to this effect. Now, Mr. Slocum and Mr. Shackford were just then at swords' points.

"I don't suppose I could annoy Shackford more," was Mr. Slocum's reflection, "than by doing something for this boy, whom he has always shamelessly neglected."

The motive was not a high one; but Richard would have been well satisfied with it, if he could have divined it. He did divine that Mr. Slocum was favorably inclined towards him, and stood watching that gentleman's face with hopeful anxiety.

"I have my regulation number of young men, Richard," said Mr. Slocum, "and there will be no vacancy until autumn. If you could wait a few months."

Richard's head drooped.

"Can't do that? You write a good hand, you say. Perhaps you could assist the book-keeper until there's a chance for you in the yard."

"I think I could, sir," said Richard eagerly.

" If you were only a draughtsman, now, I could do something much better for you. I intend to set up a shop for ornamental carving, and I want some one to draw patterns. If you had a knack at designing, if you could draw at all" -

Richard's face lighted up.

"Perhaps you *have* a turn that way. I remember the queer things you used to scratch in the mud in the court, when you were a little shaver. Can you draw?"

"Why, that is the one thing I can do!" cried Richard, - "in a rough fashion, of course," he added, fearing he had overstated it.

"It is a rough fashion that will serve. You must let me see some of your sketches."

"I haven't any, sir. I had a hundred in my sea-chest, but that was lost, - pencillings of old archways, cathedral spires, bits of frieze, and such odds and ends as took my fancy in the ports we touched at. I recollect one bit. I think I could do it for you now. Shall I?"

Mr. Slocum nodded assent, smiling at the young fellow's enthusiasm, and only partially suspecting his necessity. Richard picked up a pen and began scratching on a letter sheet which lay on the desk. He was five or six minutes at the work, during which the elder man watched him with an amused expression.

"It's a section of cornice on the façade of the Hindoo College at Calcutta," said Richard, handing him the paper, - "no, it's the custom-house. I forget which; but it doesn't matter."

The amused look gradually passed out of Mr. Slocum's countenance as he examined the sketch. It was roughly but clearly drawn, and full of facility. "Why, that's very clever!" he said, holding it at arms'-length; and then, with great gravity, "I hope you are not a genius, Richard; that would be too much of a fine thing. If you are not, you can be of service to me in my plans."

Richard laughingly made haste to declare that to the best of his knowledge and belief he was not a genius, and it was decided on the spot that Richard should assist Mr. Simms, the bookkeeper, and presently try his hand at designing ornamental patterns for the carvers, Mr. Slocum allowing him apprentice wages until the quality of his work should be ascertained.

"It is very little," said Mr. Slocum, "but it will pay your board, if you do not live at home."

"I shall not remain at my cousin's," Richard replied, "if you call that home."

"I can imagine it is not much of a home. Your cousin, not to put too fine a point on it, is a wretch."

"I am sorry to hear you say that, sir; he's my only living kinsman."

"You are fortunate in having but one, then. However, I am wrong to abuse him to you; but I cannot speak of him with moderation, he has just played me such a despicable trick. Look here."

Mr. Slocum led Richard to the door, and pointing to a row of new workshops which extended the entire length of one side of the marble yard, said, -

"I built these last spring. After the shingles were on we discovered that the rear partition, for a distance of seventy-five feet, overlapped two inches on Shackford's meadow. I was ready to drop when I saw it, your cousin is such an unmanageable old fiend. Of course I went to him immediately, and what do you think? He demanded five hundred dollars for that strip of land! Five hundred dollars for a few inches of swamp meadow not worth ten dollars the acre! 'Then take your disreputable old mill off my property!' says Shackford, - he called it a disreputable old mill! I was hasty, perhaps, and I told him to go to the devil. He said he would, and he did; for he went to Blandmann. When the lawyers got hold of it, they bothered the life out of me; so I just moved the building forward two inches, at an expense of seven hundred dollars. Then what does the demon do but board up all my windows opening on the meadow! Richard, I make it a condition that you shall not lodge at Shackford's."

"Nothing could induce me to live another day in the same house with him, sir," answered Richard, suppressing an inclination to smile; and then seriously, "His bread is bitter."

Richard went back with a light heart to Welch's Court. At the gate of the marble yard he met William Durgin returning to work. The steam-whistle had sounded the call, and there was no time for exchange of words; so Richard gave his comrade a bright nod and passed by. Durgin turned and stared after him.

"Looks as if Slocum had taken him on; but it never can be as apprentice; he wouldn't dare do it."

Mr. Shackford had nearly finished his frugal dinner when Richard entered. "If you can't hit it to be in at your meals," said Mr. Shackford, helping himself

Thomas Bailey Aldrich

absently to the remaining chop, "perhaps you had better stop away altogether."

"I can do that now, cousin," replied Richard sunnily. "I have engaged with Slocum."

The old man laid down his knife and fork.

"With Slocum! A Shackford a miserable marble-chipper!"

There was so little hint of the aristocrat in Lemuel Shackford's sordid life and person that no one suspected him of even self-esteem. He went as meanly dressed as a tramp, and as careless of contemporary criticism; yet clear down in his liver, or somewhere in his anatomy, he nourished an odd abstract pride in the family Shackford. Heaven knows why! To be sure, it dated far back; its women had always been virtuous, and its men, if not always virtuous, had always been ship-captains. But beyond this the family had never amounted to anything, and now there was so very little left of it. For Richard as Richard Lemuel cared nothing; for Richard as a Shackford he had a chaotic feeling that defied analysis and had never before risen to the surface. It was therefore with a disgust entirely apart from the hatred of Slocum or regard for Richard that the old man exclaimed, "A Shackford a miserable marble-chipper!"

"That is better than hanging around the village with my hands in my pockets. Isn't it?"

"I don't know that anybody has demanded that you should hang around the village."

"I ought to go away, you mean? But I have found work here, and I might not find it elsewhere."

"Stillwater is not the place to begin life in. It's the place to go away from, and come back to."

"Well, I have come back."

"And how? With one shirt and a lot of bad sailor habits."

"My one shirt is my only very bad habit," said Richard, with a laugh, - he could laugh now, - "and I mean to get rid of that."

Mr. Shackford snapped his fingers disdainfully.

"You ought to have stuck to the sea; that's respectable. In ten years you might have risen to be master of a bark; that would have been honorable. You might have gone down in a gale, - you probably would, - and that would have been fortunate. But a stone-cutter! You can understand," growled Mr. Shackford, reaching out for his straw hat, which he put on and crushed over his brows, "I don't keep a boarding-house for Slocum's hands."

"Oh, I'm far from asking it!" cried Richard. "I am thankful for the two nights' shelter I have had."

"That's some of your sarcasm, I suppose," said Mr. Shackford, half turning, with his hands on the door-knob.

"No, it is some of my sincerity. I am really obliged to you. You weren't very cordial, to be sure, but I did not deserve cordiality."

"You have figured that out correctly."

"I want to begin over again, you see, and start fair."

"Then begin by dropping Slocum."

"You have not given me a chance to tell you what the arrangement is. However, it's irrevocable."

"I don't want to hear. I don't care a curse, so long as it is an arrangement," and Mr. Shackford hurried out of the room, slamming the door behind him.

Then Richard, quite undisturbed by his cousin's unreasonableness, sat himself down to eat the last meal he was ever to eat under that roof, - a feat which his cousin's appetite had rendered comparatively easy.

While engaged in this, Richard resolved in his mind several questions as to his future abode. He could not reconcile his thought to any of the workingmen's boarding-houses, of which there were five or six in the slums of the village, where the doorways were greasy, and women flitted about in the hottest weather with thick woolen shawls over their heads. Yet his finances did not permit him to aspire to lodgings much more decent. If he could only secure a small room some- where in a quiet neighborhood. Possibly Mrs. Durgin would let him have a chamber in her cottage. He was beginning life over again, and it struck him as nearly an ideal plan to begin it on the identical spot where he had, in a manner, made his first start. Besides, there was William Durgin for company, when the long nights of the New England winter set in. The idea smiled so pleasantly in Richard's fancy that he pushed the plate away from him impatiently, and picked up his hat which lay on the floor beside the chair.

That evening he moved from the Shackford house to Mrs. Durgin's cottage in Cross Street. It was not an imposing ceremony. With a small brown-paper parcel under his arm, he walked from one threshold to the other, and the thing was done.

VIII

The six months which followed Richard's installment
in the office at Slocum's Yard were so crowded with
novel experience that he scarcely noted their flight.
The room at the Durgins, as will presently appear,
turned out an unfortunate arrangement; but everything
else had prospered. Richard proved an efficient aid to
Mr. Simms, who quietly shifted the pay-roll to the
younger man's shoulders. This was a very complicated
account to keep, involving as it did a separate record of
each employee's time and special work. An ancient
bookkeeper parts lightly with such trifles when he has
a capable assistant. It also fell to Richard's lot to pay
the hands on Saturdays. William Durgin blinked his
surprise on the first occasion, as he filed in with the
others and saw Richard posted at the desk, with the
pay-roll in his hand and the pile of greenbacks lying in
front of him.

"I suppose you'll be proprietor next," remarked Durgin,
that evening, at the supper table.

"When I am, Will," answered Richard cheerily, "you
will be on the road to foreman of the finishing shop."

"Thank you," said Durgin, not too graciously. It grated
on him to play the part of foreman, even in imagination, with Dick Shackford as proprietor. Durgin

could not disconnect his friend from that seedy, half-crestfallen figure to whom, a few months earlier, he had given elementary instruction on the Marble Workers' Association.

Richard did not find his old schoolmate so companionable as memory and anticipation had painted him. The two young men moved on different levels. Richard's sea life, now that he had got at a sufficient distance from it, was a perspective full of pleasant color; he had a taste for reading, a thirst to know things, and his world was not wholly shut in by the Stillwater horizon. It was still a pitifully narrow world, but wide compared with Durgin's, which extended no appreciable distance in any direction from the Stillwater hotel. He spent his evenings chiefly there, returning home late at night, and often in so noisy a mood as to disturb Richard, who slept in an adjoining apartment. This was an annoyance; and it was an annoyance to have Mrs. Durgin coming to him with complaints of William. Other matters irritated Richard. He had contrived to replenish his wardrobe, and the sunburn was disappearing from his hands, which the nature of his occupation left soft and unscarred. Durgin was disposed at times to be sarcastic on these changes, but always stopped short of actual offense; for he remembered that Shackford when a boy, amiable and patient as he was, had had a tiger's temper at bottom. Durgin had seen it roused once or twice, and even received a chance sweep of the paw. Richard liked Durgin's rough wit as little as Durgin relished Richard's good-natured bluntness. It was a mistake, that trying to pick up the dropped thread of old acquaintance.

As soon as the permanency of his position was

assured, and his means warranted the step, Richard transported himself and his effects to a comfortable chamber in the same house with Mr. Pinkham, the school-master, the perpetual falsetto of whose flute was positively soothing after four months of William Durgin's bass. Mr. Pinkham having but one lung, and that defective, played on the flute.

"You see what you've gone and done, William," remarked Mrs. Durgin plaintively, "with your ways. There goes the quietest young man in Stillwater, and four dollars a week!"

"There goes a swell, you'd better say. He was always a proud beggar; nobody was ever good enough for him."

"You shouldn't say that, William. I could cry, to lose him and his cheerfulness out of the house," and Mrs. Durgin began to whimper.

"Wait till he's out of luck again, and he'll come back to us fast enough. That's when his kind remembers their friends. Blast him! He can't even take a drop of beer with a chum at the tavern."

"And right, too. There's beer enough taken at the tavern without him."

"If you mean me, mother, I'll get drunk tonight."

"No, no!" cried Mrs. Durgin, pleadingly, "I didn't mean you, William, but Peters and that set."

"I thought you couldn't mean me," said William, thrusting his hands into the pockets of his monkey-jacket, and sauntering off in the direction of the

Stillwater hotel, where there was a choice company gathered, it being Saturday night, and the monthly meeting of the Union.

Mr. Slocum had wasted no time in organizing a shop for his experiment in ornamental carving. Five or six men, who had worked elsewhere at this branch, were turned over to the new department, with Stevens as foreman and Richard as designer. Very shortly Richard had as much as he could do to furnish the patterns required. These consisted mostly of scrolls, wreaths, and mortuary dove-wings for head-stones. Fortunately for Richard he had no genius, but plenty of a kind of talent just abreast with Mr. Slocum's purpose. As the carvers became interested in their work, they began to show Richard the respect and good-will which at first had been withheld, for they had not quite liked being under the supervision of one who had not served at the trade. His youth had also told against him; but Richard's pleasant, off-hand manner quickly won them. He had come in contact with rough men on shipboard; he had studied their ways, and he knew that with all their roughness there is no class so sensitive. This insight was of great service to him. Stevens, who had perhaps been the least disposed to accept Richard, was soon his warm ally.

"See what a smooth fist the lad has!" he said one day holding up a new drawing to the shop. "A man with a wreath of them acorns on his head-stone oughter be perfectly happy, damn him!"

It was, however, an anchor with a broken chain pendent - a design for a monument to the late Captain Septimius Salter, who had parted his cable at sea - which settled Richard's status with Stevens.

"Boys, that Shackford is what I call a born genei."

After all, is not the one-eyed man who is king among the blind the most fortunate of monarchs? Your little talent in a provincial village looms a great deal taller than your mighty genius in a city. Richard Whackford working for Rowland Slocum at Stillwater was happier than Michaelangelo in Rome with Pope Julius II. at his back. And Richard was the better paid, too!

One day he picked up a useful hint from a celebrated sculptor, who had come to the village in search of marble for the base of a soldiers' monument. Richard was laboriously copying a spray of fern, the delicacy of which eluded his pencil. The sculptor stood a moment silently observing him.

"Why do you spend an hour doing only passably well what you could do perfectly in ten minutes?"

"I suppose it is because I am stupid, sir," said Richard.

"No stupid man ever suspected himself of being anything but clever. You can draw capitally; but nature beats you out and out at designing ferns. Just ask her to make you a fac-simile in plaster, and see how handily she will lend herself to the job. Of course you must help her a little."

"Oh, I am not above giving nature a lift," said Richard modestly.

"Lay a cloth on your table, place the fern on the cloth, and pour a thin paste of plaster of Paris over the leaf, - do that gently, so as not to disarrange the spray. When the plaster is set, there's your mold; remove the leave, oil the matrix, and pour in fresh plaster. When that is set, cut away tdhe mold carefully, and there's your spray of fern, as graceful and perfect as if nature had done it all by herself. You get the very texture of the leaf by this process."

After that, Richard made casts instead of drawings for the carvers, and fancied he was doing a new thing, until he visited some marble-works in the great city.

At this period, whatever change subsequently took place in his feeling, Richard was desirous of establishing friendly relations with his cousin. The young fellow's sense of kinship was singularly strong, and it was only after several repulses at the door of the Shackford house and on the street that he relinquished the hope of placating the sour old man. At times Richard was moved almost to pity him. Every day Mr. Shackford seemed to grow shabbier and more spectral. He was a grotesque figure now, in his napless hat and broken-down stock. The metal button-holes on his ancient waistcoat had worn their way through the satin coverings, leaving here and there a sparse fringe around the edges, and somehow suggesting little bald heads. Looking at him, you felt that the inner man was as threadbare and dilapidated as his outside; but in his lonely old age he asked for no human sympathy or companionship, and, in fact, stood in no need of either. With one devouring passion he set the world at defiance. He loved his gold, - the metal itself, the weight an color and touch of it. In his bedroom on the ground-floor Mr. Shackford kept a small iron-clamped box filled to the lid with bright yellow coins. Often, at the dead of night, with door bolted and curtain down, he would spread out the glittering pieces on the table, and bend over them with an amorous glow in his faded

Thomas Bailey Aldrich

eyes. These were his blond mistresses; he took a fearful joy in listening to their rustling, muffle laughter as he drew them towards him with eager hands. If at that instant a blind chanced to slam, or a footfall to echo in the lonely court, then the withered old sultan would hurry his slaves back into their iron-bound seraglio, and extinguish the light. It would have been a wasted tenderness to pity him. He was very happy in his own way, that Lemuel Shackford.

IX

Towards the close of his second year with Mr. Slocum, Richard was assigned a work-room by himself, and relieved of his accountant's duties. His undivided energies were demanded by the carving department, which had proved a lucrative success.

The rear of the lot on which Mr. Slocum's house stood was shut off from the marble yard by a high brick wall pierced with a private door for Mr. Slocum's convenience. Over the kitchen in the extension, which reached within a few feet of the wall, was a disused chamber, approachable on the outside by a flight of steps leading to a veranda. To this room Richard and his traps were removed. With a round table standing in the center, with the plaster models arranged on shelves and sketches in pencil and crayon tacked against the whitewashed walls, the apartment was transformed into a delightful atelier. An open fire-place, with a brace of antiquated iron-dogs straddling the red brick hearth, gave the finishing touch. The occupant was in easy communication with the yard, from which the busy din of clinking chisels came u musically to his ear, and was still beyond the reach of unnecessary interruption. Richard saw clearly all the advantages of this transfer, but he was far form having any intimation that he had made the most important move of his life.

The room had two doors: one opened on the veranda, and the other into a narrow hall connecting the extension with the main building. Frequently, that first week after taking possession, Richard detected the sweep of a broom and the rustle of drapery in this passage-way, the sound sometimes hushing itself quite close to the door, as if some one had paused a moment just outside. He wondered whether it was the servant-maid or Margaret Slocum, whom he knew very well by sight. It was, in fact, Margaret, who was dying with the curiosity of fourteen to peep into the studio, so carefully locked whenever the young man left it, - dying with curiosity to see the workshop, and standing in rather great awe of the workman.

In the home circle her father had a habit of speaking with deep respect of young Shackford's ability, and once she had seen him at their table, - at a Thanks-giving. On this occasion Richard had appalled her by the solemnity of his shyness, - poor Richard, who was so unused to the amenities of a handsomely served dinner, that the chill which came over him cooled the Thanksgiving turkey on his palate.

When it had been decided that he was to have the spare room for his workshop, Margaret, with womanly officiousness, had swept it and dusted it and demoli-shed the cobwebs; but since then she had not been able to obtain so much as a glimpse of the interior. A ten minutes' sweeping had sufficed for the chamber, but the passage-way seemed in quite an irreclaimable state, judging by the number of times it was necessary to sweep it in the course of a few days. Now Margaret was not an unusual mixture of timidity and daring; so one morning, about a week after Richard was settled, she walked with quaking heart up to the door of the studio, and knocked as bold as brass.

Richard opened the door, and smiled pleasantly at Margaret standing on the threshold with an expression of demure defiance in her face. Did Mr. Shackford want anything more in the way of pans and pails for his plaster? No, Mr. Shackford had everything he required of the kind. But would not Miss Margaret walk in? Yes, she would step in for a moment, but with a good deal of indifference, though, giving an air of chance to her settled determination to examine that room from top to bottom.

Richard showed her his drawings and casts, and enlightened her on all the simple mysteries of the craft. Margaret, of whom he was a trifle afraid at first, amused him with her candor and sedateness, seeming now a mere child, and now an elderly person gravely inspecting matters. The frankness and simplicity were hers by nature, and the oldish ways - notably her self-possession, so quick to assert itself after an instant's forgetfulness - came perhaps of losing her mother in early childhood, and the premature duties which that misfortune entailed. She amused him, for she was only fourteen; but she impressed him also, for she was Mr. Slocum's daughter. Yet it was not her lightness, but her gravity, that made Richard smile to himself.

"I am not interrupting you?" she asked presently.

"Not in the least," said Richard. "I am waiting for these molds to harden. I cannot do anything until then."

"Papa says you are very clever," remarked Margaret, turning her wide black eyes full upon him. *"Are* you?"

"Far from it," replied Richard, laughing to veil his confusion, "but I am glad your father thinks so."

"You should not be glad to have him think so," returned Margaret reprovingly, "if you are not clever. I suppose you are, though. Tell the truth, now."

"It is not fair to force a fellow into praising himself."

"You are trying to creep out!"

"Well, then, there are many cleverer persons than I in the world, and a few not so clever."

"That won't do," said Margaret positively.

"I don't understand what you mean by cleverness, Miss Margaret. There are a great many kinds and degrees. I can make fairly honest patterns for the men to work by; but I am not an artist, if you mean that."

"You are not an artist?"

"No; an artist creates, and I only copy, and that in a small way. Any one can learn to prepare casts; but to create a bust or a statue - that is to say, a fine one - a man must have genius."

"You have no genius?"

"Not a grain."

"I am sorry to hear that," said Margaret, with a disappointed look. "But perhaps it will come," she added encouragingly. "I have read that nearly all great artists and poets are almost always modest. They know better than anybody else how far they fall short of what they intend, and so they don't put on airs. You don't, either. I like that in you. May be you have genius without knowing it, Mr. Shackford."

"It is quite without knowing it, I assure you!" protested Richard, with suppressed merriment. "What an odd girl!" he thought. "She is actually talking to me like a mother!"

The twinkling light in the young man's eyes, or something that jarred in his manner, caused Margaret at once to withdraw into herself. She went silently about the room, examining the tools and patterns; then, nearing the door, suddenly dropped Richard a quaint little courtesy, and was gone.

This was the colorless beginning of a friendship that was destined speedily to be full of tender lights and shadows, and to flow on with unsuspected depth. For several days Richard saw nothing more of Margaret, and scarcely thought of her. The strangle little figure was fading out of his mind, when, one afternoon, it again appeared at his door. This time Margaret had left something of her sedateness behind; she struck Richard as being both less ripe and less immature than he had fancied; she interested rather than amused him. Perhaps he had been partially insulated by his own shyness on the first occasion, and had caught only a confused and inaccurate impression of Margaret's personality. She remained half an hour in the workshop, and at her departure omitted the formal courtesy.

After this, Margaret seldom let a week slip without tapping once or twice at the studio, at first with some pretext or other, and then with no pretense whatever. When Margaret had disburdened herself of excuses for dropping in to watch Richard mold his leaves and flowers, she came oftener, and Richard insensibly drifted into the habit of expecting her on certain days, and was disappointed when she failed to appear. His industry had saved him, until now, from discovering how solitary his life really was; for his life was as solitary - as solitary as that of Margaret, who lived in the great house with only her father, the two servants, and an episodical aunt. The mother was long ago dead; Margaret could not recollect when that gray headstone, with blotches of rusty-green moss breaking out over the lettering, was not in the churchyard; and there never had been any brothers or sisters.

To Margaret Richard's installation in the empty room, where as a child she had always been afraid to go, was the single important break she could remember in the monotony of her existence; and now a vague yearning for companionship, the blind sense of the plant reaching towards the sunshine, drew her there. The tacitly prescribed half hour often lengthened to an hour. Sometimes Margaret brought a book with her, or a piece of embroidery, and the two spoke scarcely ten words, Richard giving her a smile now and then, and she returning a sympathetic nod as the cast came out successfully.

Margaret at fifteen - she was fifteen now - was not a beauty. There is the loveliness of the bud and the loveliness of the full-blown flower; but Margaret as a blossom was not pretty. She was awkward and angular, with prominent shoulder-blades, and no soft curves anywhere in her slimness; only her black hair, growing low on the forehead, and her eyes were fine. Her profile, indeed, with the narrow forehead and the sensitive upper lip, might fairly have suggested the mask of Clytie which Richard had bought of an itinerant image-dealer, and fixed on a bracket over the mantel-shelf. But her eyes were her specialty, if one may say that. They were fringed with such heavy lashes that the girl seemed always to be in half-mourning. Her smile was singularly sweet and bright, perhaps because it broke through so much somber coloring.

If there was a latent spark of sentiment between Richard and Margaret in those earlier days, neither was conscious of it; they had seemingly begun where happy lovers generally end, - by being dear comrades. He liked to have Margaret sitting there, with her needle flashing in the sunlight, or her eyelashes making a rich gloom above the book as she read aloud. It was so agreeable to look up from his work, and not be alone. He had been alone so much. And Margaret found nothing in the world pleasanter than to sit there and watch Richard making his winter garden, as she called it. By and by it became her custom to pass every Saturday afternoon in that employment.

Margaret was not content to be merely a visitor; she took a housewifely care of the workshop, resolutely straightening out its chronic disorder at unexpected moments, and fighting the white dust that settled upon everything. The green-paper shade, which did not roll up very well, at the west window was of her devising. An empty camphor vial on Richard's desk had always a clove pink, or a pansy, or a rose, stuck into it, according to the season. She hid herself away and peeped out in a hundred feminine things in the room. Sometimes she was a bit of crochet-work left on a chair, and sometimes she was only a hair-pin, which Richard gravely picked up and put on the mantel-piece.

Mr. Slocum threw no obstacles in the path of this idyllic friendship; possibly he did not observe it. In his eyes Margaret was still a child, - a point of view that necessarily excluded any consideration of Richard. Perhaps, however, if Mr. Slocum could have assisted invisibly at a pretty little scene which took place in the studio, one day, some twelve or eighteen months after Margaret's first visit to it, he might have found food for reflection.

It was a Saturday afternoon. Margaret had come into the workshop with her sewing, as usual. The papers on the round table had been neatly cleared away, and Richard was standing by the window, indolently drumming on the glass with a palette-knife.

"Not at work this afternoon?"

"I was waiting for you."

"That is no excuse at all," said Margaret, sweeping across the room with a curious air of self-conscious-ness, and arranging her drapery with infinite pains as she seated herself.

Richard looked puzzled for a moment, and then exclaimed, "Margaret, you have got on a long dress!"

"Yes," said Margaret, with dignity. "Do you like it, - the train?"

"That's a train?"

"Yes," said Margaret, standing up and glancing over her left shoulder at the soft folds of maroon-colored stuff, which, with a mysterious feminine movement of the foot, she caused to untwist itself and flow out gracefully behind her. There was really something very pretty in the hesitating lines of the tall, slender figure, as she leaned back that way. Certain unsuspected points emphasized themselves so cunningly.

"I never saw anything finer," declared Richard. "It was worth waiting for."

"But you shouldn't have waited," said Margaret, with a gratified flush, settling herself into the chair again. "It was understood that you were never to let me interfere with your work."

"You see you have, by being twenty minutes late. I've finished that acorn border for Stevens's capitals, and there's nothing more to do for the yard. I am going to make something for myself, and I want you to lend me a hand."

"How can I help you, Richard?" Margaret asked, promptly stopping the needle in the hem.

"I need a paper-weight to keep my sketches from being blown about, and I wish you literally to lend me a hand, - a hand to take a cast of."

"Really?"

"I think that little white claw would make a very neat paper-weight," said Richard.

Margaret gravely rolled up her sleeve to the elbow, and

contemplated the hand and wrist critically.

"It is like a claw, isn't it. I think you can find some-thing better than that."

"No; that is what I want, and nothing else. That, or no paper-weight for me."

"Very well, just as you choose. It will be a fright."

"The other hand, please."

"I gave you the left because I've a ring on this one."

"You can take off the ring, I suppose."

"Of course I can take it off."

"Well, then, do."

"Richard," said Margaret severely, "I hope you are not a fidget."

"A what?"

"A fuss, then, - a person who always wants everything some other way, and makes just twice as much trouble as anybody else."

"No, Margaret, I am not that. I prefer your right hand because the left is next to the heart, and the evaporation of the water in the plaster turns it as cold as snow. Your arm will be chilled to the shoulder. We don't want to do anything to hurt the good little heart, you know."

"Certainly not," said Margaret. "There!" and she rested her right arm on the table, while Richard placed the hand in the desired position on a fresh napkin which he had folded for the purpose.

"Let your hand lie flexible, please. Hold it naturally. Why do you stiffen the fingers so?"

"I don't; they stiffen themselves, Richard. They know they are going to have their photograph taken, and can't look natural. Who ever does?"

After a minute the fingers relaxed, and settled of their own accord into an easy pose. Richard laid his hand softly on her wrist.

"Don't move now."

"I'll be as quiet as a mouse," said Margaret giving a sudden queer little glance at his face.

Richard emptied a paper of white powder into a great yellow bowl half filled with water and fell to stirring it vigorously, like a pastry-cook beating eggs. When the plaster was of the proper consistency he began building it up around the hand, pouring on a spoonful at a time, here and there, carefully. In a minute or two the inert white fingers were completely buried. Margaret made a comical grimace.

"Is it cold?"

"Ice," said Margaret, shutting her eyes involuntarily.

"If it is too disagreeable we can give it up," suggested Richard.

"No, don't touch it!" she cried, waving him back with her free arm. "I don't mind; but it's as cold as so much snow. How curious! What does it?"

"I suppose a scientific fellow could explain the matter to you easily enough. When the water evaporates a kind of congealing process sets in, - a sort of atmospheric change, don't you know? The sudden precipitation of the - the" -

"You're as good as Tyndall on Heat," said Margaret demurely.

"Oh, Tyndall is well enough in his way," returned Richard, "but of course he doesn't go into things so deeply as I do."

"The idea of telling me that 'a congealing process set in,' when I am nearly frozen to death!" cried Margaret, bowing her head over the imprisoned arm.

"Your unseemly levity, Margaret, makes it necessary for me to defer my remarks on natural phenomena until some more fitting occasion."

"Oh, Richard, don't let an atmospherical change come over *you!*"

"When you knocked at my door, months ago," said Richard, "I didn't dream you were such a satirical little piece, or may be you wouldn't have got in. You stood there as meek as Moses, with your frock reaching only to the tops of your boots. You were a deception, Margaret."

"I was dreadfully afraid of you, Richard."

"You are not afraid of me nowadays."

"Not a bit."

"You are showing your true colors. That long dress, too! I believe the train has turned your head."

"But just now you said you admired it."

"So I did, and do. It makes you look quite like a woman, though."

"I want to be a woman. I would like to be as old - as old as Mrs. Methuselah. Was there a Mrs. Methuselah?"

"I really forget," replied Richard, considering. "But there must have been. The old gentleman had time enough to have several. I believe, however, that history is rather silent about his domestic affairs."

"Well, then," said Margaret, after thinking it over, "I would like to be as old as the youngest Mrs. Methuselah."

"That was probably the last one," remarked Richard, with great profundity. "She was probably some giddy young thing of seventy or eighty. Those old widowers never take a wife of their own age. I shouldn't want you to be seventy, Margaret, - or even eighty."

"On the whole, perhaps, I shouldn't fancy it myself. Do you approve of persons marrying twice?"

"N - o, not at the same time."

"Of course I didn't mean that," said Margaret, with asperity. "How provoking you can be!"

"But they used to, - in the olden time, don't you know?"

"No, I don't."

Richard burst out laughing. "Imagine him," he cried, - "imagine Methuselah in his eight or nine hundredth year, dressed in his customary bridal suit, with a sprig of century-plant stuck in his button-hole!"

"Richard," said Margaret solemnly, "you shouldn't speak jestingly of a scriptural character."

At this Richard broke out again. "But gracious me!" he exclaimed, suddenly checking himself. "I am forgetting you all this while!"

Richard hurriedly reversed the mass of plaster on the table, and released Margaret's half-petrified fingers. They were shriveled and colorless with the cold.

"There isn't any feeling in it whatever," said Margaret, holding up her hand helplessly, like a wounded wing.

Richard took the fingers between his palms, and chafed them smartly for a moment or two to restore the suspended circulation.

"There, that will do," said Margaret, withdrawing her hand.

"Are you all right now?"

"Yes, thanks;" and then she added, smiling, "I suppose a scientific fellow could explain why my fingers seem to be full of hot pins and needles shooting in every direction."

"Tyndall's your man - Tyndall on Heat," answered Richard, with a laugh, turning to examine the result of his work. "The mold is perfect, Margaret. You were a good girl to keep so still."

Richard then proceeded to make the cast, which was soon placed on the window ledgde to harden in the sun. When the plaster was set, he cautiously chipped off the shell with a chisel, Margaret leaning over his shoulder to watch the operation, - and there was the little white claw, which ever after took such dainty care of his papers, and ultimately became so precious to him as a part of Margaret's very self that he would not have exchanged it for the Venus of Milo.

But as yet Richard was far enough from all that.

Thomas Bailey Aldrich

X

Three years glided by with Richard Shackford as swiftly as those periods of time which are imagined to elapse between the acts of a play. They were eventless, untroubled years, and have no history. Nevertheless, certain changes had taken place. Little by little Mr. Slocum had relinquished the supervision of the work-shops to Richard, until now the affairs of the yard rested chiefly on his shoulders. It was like a dream to him when he looked directly back to his humble beginning, though as he reflected upon it, and retraced his progress step by step, he saw there was nothing illogical or astonishing in his good fortune. He had won it by downright hard work and the faithful exercise of a sufficing talent.

In his relations with Margaret, Richard's attitude had undergone no appreciable change. Her chance visits to the studio through the week and those pleasant, half-idle Saturday afternoons had become to both Richard and Margaret a matter of course, like the sunlight, or the air they breathed.

To Richard, Margaret Slocum at nineteen was simply a charming, frank girl, - a type of gracious young womanhood. He was conscious of her influence; he was very fond of Margaret; but she had not yet taken on for him that magic individuality which makes a woman the one woman in the world to her lover. Though Richard had scant experience in such matters, he was not wrong in accepting Margaret as the type of a class of New England girls, which, fortunately for New England, is not a small class. These young women for the most part lead quiet and restricted lives so far as the actualities are concerned, but very deep and full lives in the world of books and imagination, to which they make early escapes. They have the high instincts that come of good blood, the physique that naturally fits fine manners; and when chance takes one of these maidens from her island country home or from some sleepy town on the sea-board, and sets her amid the complications of city existence, she is an unabashed and unassuming lady. If in Paris, she differs from the Parisiennes only in the greater delicacy of her lithe beauty, her innocence which is not ignorance, and her French pronunciation; if in London, she differs from English girls only in the matter of rosy cheeks and the rising inflection. Should none of these fortunate transplantings befall her, she always merits them by adorning with grace and industry and intelligence the narrower sphere to which destiny has assigned her.

Destiny had assigned Margaret Slocum to a very narrow sphere; it had shut her up in an obscure New England manufacturing village, with no society, strictly speaking, and no outlets whatever to large experiences. To her father's affection, Richard's friendship, and her household duties she was forced to look for her happiness. If life held wider possibilities for her, she had not dreamed of them. She looked up to Richard with respect, - perhaps with a dash of sentiment in the respect; there was something at once gentle and virile in his character which she admired and leaned upon; in his presence the small house-keeping troubles always slipped from her; but her heart, to use a pretty French phrase, had not consciously spoken, - possibly it had murmured a little, incoherently, to itself, but it had not spoken out aloud, as perhaps it would have done long ago if an impediment had been placed in the way of their intimacy. With all her subtler intuitions, Margaret was as far as Richard from suspecting the strength and direction of the current with which they were drifting. Freedom, habit, and the nature of their environment conspired to prolong this mutual lack of perception. The hour had sounded, however, when these two were to see each other in a different light.

One Monday morning in March, at the close of the three years in question, as Richard mouinted the outside staircase leading to his studio in the extension, the servant-maid beckoned to him from the kitchen window.

Margaret had failed to come to the studio the previous Saturday afternoon. Richard had worked at cross-purposes and returned to his boarding-house vaguely dissatisfied, as always happened to him on those rare occasions when she missed the appointment; but he had thought little of the circumstance. Nor had he been disturbed on Sunday at seeing the Slocum pew vacant during both services. The heavy snow-storm which had begun the night before accounted for at least Margaret's absence.

"Mr. Slocum told me to tell you that he shouldn't be in the yard to-day," said the girl. "Miss Margaret is very ill."

"Ill!" Richard repeated, and the smile with which he had leaned over the rail towards the window went out instantly on his lip.

"Dr. Weld was up with her until five o'clock this morning," said the girl, fingering the corner of her apron. "She's that low."

"What is the matter?"

"It's a fever."

"What kind of fever?"

"I don't mind me what the doctor called it. He thinks it come from something wrong with the drains."

"He didn't say typhoid?"

"Yes, that's the name of it."

Richard ascended the stairs with a slow step, and a moment afterwards stood stupidly in the middle of the workshop. "Margaret is going to die," he said to himself, giving voice to the dark foreboding that had instantly seized upon him, and in a swift vision he saw the end of all that simple, fortunate existence which he had lived without once reflecting it could ever end. He mechanically picked up a tool from the table, and laid it down again. Then he seated himself on the low bench between the windows. It was Margaret's favorite place; it was not four days since she sat there reading to him. Already it appeared long ago, - years and years ago. He could hardly remember when he did not have this heavy weight on his heart. His life of yesterday abruptly presented itself to him as a reminiscence; he saw now how happy that life had been, and how lightly he had accepted it. It took to itself all that precious quality of things irrevocably lost.

The clamor of the bell in the South Church striking noon, and the shrilling of the steam-whistle softened by the thick-falling snow, roused Richard from his abstraction. He was surprised that it was noon. He rose from the bench and went home through the storm, scarcely heeding the sleet that snapped in his face like whip-lashes. Margaret was going to die!

 For four or five seeks the world was nearly a blank to Richard Shackford. The insidious fever that came and went, bringing alternate despair and hope to the watchers in the hushed room, was in his veins also. He passed the days between his lonely lodgings in Lime Street and the studio, doing nothing, restless and apathetic by turns, but with always a poignant sense of anxiety. He ceased to take any distinct measurement of time further than to note that an interval of months seemed to separate Monday from Monday. Meanwhile, if new patterns had been required by the men, the work in the carving departments would have come to a dead lock.

At length the shadow lifted, and there fell a day of soft May weather when Margaret, muffled in shawls and as white as death, was seated once more in her accustomed corner by the west window. She had insisted on being brought there the first practicable moment; nowhere else in the house was such sunshine, and Mr. Slocum himself had brought her in his arms. She leaned back against the pillows, smiling faintly. Her fingers lay locked on her lap, and the sunlight showed through the narrow transparent palace. It was as if her hands were full of blush-roses.

Richard breathed again, but not with so free a heart as before. What if she had died? He felt an immense pity for himself when he thought of that, and he thought of it continually as the days wore on.

Either a great alteration had wrought itself in Margaret, or Richard beheld her through a clearer medium during the weeks of convalescence that followed. Was this the slight, sharp-faced girl he used to know? The eyes and the hair were the same; but the smile was deeper, and the pliant figure had lost its extreme slimness without a sacrifice to its delicacy. The spring air was filling her veins with abundant health, and mantling her cheeks with a richer duskiness than they had ever worn. Margaret was positively handsome. Her beauty had come all in a single morning, like the crocuses. This beauty began to awe Richard; it had the effect of seeming to remove her further and further from him. He grew moody and restless when they were together, and was wretched alone. His constraint did not escape Margaret. She watched him, and wondered at his inexplicable depression when every one in the household was rejoicing in her recovery. By and by this depression wounded her, but she was too spirited to show the hurt. She always brought a book with her now, in her visits to the studio; it was less awkward to read than to sit silent and unspoken to over a piece of needle-work.

"How very odd you are!" said Margaret, one afternoon, closing the volume which she had held mutely for several minutes, waiting for Richard to grasp the fact that she was reading aloud.

"I odd!" protested Richard, breaking with a jerk from one of his long reveries. "In what way?"

"As if I could explain - when you put the quotation suddenly, like that."

"I didn't intend to be abrupt. I was curious to know. And then the charge itself was a trifle unexpected, if you will look at it. But never mind," he added with a smile; "think it over, and tell me to-morrow."

"No, I will tell you now, since you are willing to wait."

"I wasn't really willing to wait, but I knew if I didn't pretend to be I should never get it out of you."

"Very well, then; your duplicity is successful. Richard, I was puzzled whre to begin with your oddities."

"Begin at the beginning."

"No, I will take the nearest. When a young lady is affable enough to read aloud to you, the least you can do is to listen to her. That is a deference you owe to the author, when it happens to be Hawthorne, to say nothing of the young lady."

"But I *have* been listening, Margaret. Every word!"

"Where did I leave off?"

"It was where - where the" - and Richard knitted his brows in the vain effort to remember - "where the young daguerreotypist, what's-his-name, took up his residence in the House of the Seven Gables."

"No, sir! You stand convicted. It was ten pages further on. The last words were," - and Margaret read from the book, -

"'Good-night, cousin,' said Phoebe, strangely affected by Hepsibah's manner. 'If you being to love me, I am glad.'"

"There, sir! what do you say to that?"

Richard did not say anything, but he gave a guilty start, and shot a rapid glance at Margaret coolly enjoying her triumph.

"In the next place," she continued soberly, after a pause, "I think it very odd in you not to reply to me, - oh, not now, for of course you are without a word of justification; but at other times. Frequently, when I speak to you, you look at me so," making a vacant little face, "and then suddenly disappear, - I don't mean bodily, but mentally."

"I am no great talker at best," said Richard with a helpless air. "I seldom speak unless I have something to say."

"But other people do. I, for instance."

"Oh, you, Margaret; that is different. When you talk I don't much mind what you are talking about."

"I like a neat, delicate compliment like that!"

"What a perverse girl you are to-day!" cried Richard. "You won't understand me. I mean that your words and your voice are so pleasant they make anything

Thomas Bailey Aldrich

interesting, whether it's important or not."

"If no one were to speak until he had something important to communicate," observed Margaret, "conversation in this world would come to a general stop." Then she added, with a little ironical smile, "Even you, Richard, wouldn't be talking all the time."

Formerly Margaret's light sarcasms, even when the struck him point-blank, used to amuse Richard, but now he winced at being merely grazed.

Margaret went on: "But it's not a bit necessary to be circular or instructive - with me. I am interested in trivial matters, - in the weather, in my spring hat, in what you are going to do next, and the like. One must occupy one's self with something. But you, Richard, nowadays you seem interested in nothing, and have nothing whatever to say."

Poor Richard! He had a great deal to say, but he did not know how, nor if it were wise to breathe it. Just three little words, murmured or whispered, and the whole conditions would be changed. With those fateful words uttered, what would be Margaret's probable attitude, and what Mr. Sclocum's? Though the line which formerly drew itself between employer and employee had grown faint with time, it still existed in Richard's mind, and now came to the surface with great distinctness, like a word written in sympathetic ink. If he spoke, and Margaret was startled or offended, then there was an end to their free, unembarrassed intercourse, - perhaps an end to all intercourse. By keeping his secret in his breast he at least secured the present. But that was to risk everything. Any day somebody might come and carry

Margaret off under his very eyes. As he reflected on this, the shadow of John Dana, the son of the rich iron-manufacturer, etched itself sharply upon Richard's imagination. Within the week young Dana had declared in the presence of Richard that "Margaret Slocum was an awfully nice little thing," and the Othello in Richard's blood had been set seething. Then his thought glanced from John Dana to Mr. Pinkham and the Rev. Arthur Langly, both of whom were assiduous visitors at the house. The former had lately taken to accompanying Margaret on the piano with his dismal little flute, and the latter was perpetually making a moth of himself about her class at Sunday-school.

Richard stood with the edge of his chisel resting idly upon the plaster mold in front of him, pondering these things. Presently he heard Margaret's voice, as if somewhere in the distance, saying, -

"I have not finished yet, Richard."

"Go on," said Richard, falling to work again with a kind of galvanic action. "Go on, please."

"I have a serious grievance. Frankly, I am hurt by your preoccupation and indifference, your want of openness or cordiality, - I don't know how to name it. You are the only person who seems to be unaware that I escaped a great danger a month ago. I am obliged to remember all the agreeable hours I have spent in the studio to keep off the impression that during my illness you got used to not seeing me, and that now my presence somehow obstructs your work and annoys you."

Richard threw his chisel on the bench, and crossed over to the window where Margaret was.

"You are as wrong as you can be," he said, looking down on her half-lifted face, from which a quick wave of color was subsiding; for the abruptness of Richard's movement had startled her.

"I am glad if I am wrong."

"It is nearly an unforgivable thing to be as wide of the mark as you are. Oh, Margaret, if you had died that time!"

"You would have been very sorry?"

"Sorry? No. That doesn't express it; one outlives mere sorrow. If anything had happened to you, I should never have got over it. You don't know what those five weeks were to me. It was a kind of death to come to this room day after day, and not find you."

Margaret rested her eyes thoughtfully on the space occupied by Richard rather than on Richard himself, seeming to look through and beyond him, as if he were incorporeal.

"You missed me like that?" she said slowly.

"I missed you like that."

Margaret meditated a moment. "In the first days of my illness I wondered if you didn't miss me a little; afterwards everything was confused in my mind. When I tried to think, I seemed to be somebody else, - I seemed to be *you* waiting for me here in the studio.

Wasn't that singular? But when I recovered, and returned to my old place, I began to suspect I had been bearing your anxiety, - that I had been distressed by the absence to which you had grown accustomed."

"I never got used to it, Margaret. It became more and more unendurable. This workshop was full of - of your absence. There wasn't a sketch or a cast or an object in the room that didn't remind me of you, and seem to mock at me for having let the most precious moments of my life slip away unheeded. That bit of geranium in the glass yonder seemed to say with its dying breath, 'You have cared for neither of us as you ought to have cared; my scent and her goodness have been all one to you, - things to take or to leave. It was for no merit of yours that she was always planning something to make life smoother and brighter for you. What had you done to deserve it? How unselfish and generous and good she has been to you for years and years! What would have become of you without her? She left me here on purpose' - it's the geranium leaf that is speaking all the while, Margaret - 'to say this to you, and to tell you that she was not half appreciated; but now you have lost her.'"

As she leaned forward listening, with her lips slightly parted, Margaret gave an unconscious little approbative nod of the head. Richard's fanciful accusation of himself caused her a singular thrill of pleasure. He had never before spoken to her in just this fashion; the subterfuge which his tenderness had employed, the little detour it had made in order to get at her, was a novel species of flattery. She recognized the ring of a distinctly new note in his voice; but, strangely enough, the note lost its unfamiliarity in an instant. Margaret recognized that fact also, and as she swiftly speculate don the phenomenon her pulse went one or two strokes faster.

"Oh, you poor boy!" she said, looking up with a laugh, and a flush so interfused that they seemed one, "that geranium took a great deal upon itself. It went quite beyond its instructions, which were simply to remind you of me now and then. One day, while you were out, - the day before I was taken ill, - I placed the flowers on the desk there, perhaps with a kind of premonition that I was going away from you for a time."

"What if you had never come back?"

"I wouldn't think of that if I were you," said Margaret softly.

"But it haunts me, - that thought. Sometimes of a morning, after I unlock the workshop door, I stand hesitating, with my hand on the latch, as one might hesitate a few seconds before stepping into a tomb. There were days last month, Margaret, when this chamber did appear to me like a tomb. All that was happy in my past seemed to lie buried here; it was something visible and tangible; I used to steal in and look upon it."

"Oh, Richard!"

"If you only knew what a life I led as a boy in my cousin's house, and what a doleful existence for years afterwards, until I found, perhaps you would understand my despair when I saw everything suddenly slipping away from me. Margaret! the day your father brought you in here, I had all I could do not to kneel down at your feet" - Richard stopped short. "I didn't mean to tell you that," he added, turning towards the work-table. Then he checked himself, and came and stood in front of her again. He had gone too far not to go further. "While you were ill I made a great discovery."

"What was that, Richard?"

"I discovered that I had been blind for two or three years."

"Blind?" repeated Margaret.

"Stone-blind. I discovered it by suddenly seeing - by seeing that I had loved you all the while, Margaret! Are you offended?"

"No," said Margaret, slowly; she was a moment finding her voice to say it. "I - ought I to be offended?"

"Not if you are not!" said Richard.

"Then I am note. I - I've made little discoveries myself," murmured Margaret, going into full mourning with her eyelashes.

But it was only for an instant. She refused to take her happiness shyly or insincerely; it was something too sacred. She was a trifle appalled by it, if the truth must be told. If Richard had scattered his love-making through the month of her convalescence, or if he had made his avowal in a different mood, perhaps Margaret might have met him with some natural coquetry. But Richard's tone and manner had been such as to suppress any instinct of the kind. His declaration, moreover, had amazed her. Margaret's own feelings had been more or less plain to her that past month, and she had diligently disciplined herself to accept Richard's friendship, since it seemed all he had to give. Indeed, it had seemed at times as if he had not even that.

When Margaret lifted her eyes to him, a second after her confession, they were full of a sweet seriousness, and she had no thought of withdrawing the hands which Richard had taken, and was holding lightly, that she might withdraw them if she willed. She felt no impulse to do so, though as Margaret looked up she saw her father standing a few paces behind Richard.

With an occult sense of another presence in the room, Richard, turned at the same instant.

Mr. Slocum had advanced two steps into the apartment, and had been brought to a dead halt by the surprising tableau in the embrasure of the window. He stood motionless, with an account-book under his arm, while a dozen expressions chased each other over his countenance.

"Mr. Slocum," said Richard, who saw that only one course lay open to him, "I love Margaret, and I have been telling her."

At that the flitting shadows on Mr. Slocum's face settled into one grave look. He did not reply immediately, but let his glance wander from Margaret to Richard, and back again to Margaret, slowly digesting the fact. It was evident he had not relished it. Meanwhile the girl had risen from the chair and was moving towards her father.

"This strikes me as very extraordinary," he said at last. "You have never given any intimation that such a feeling existed. How long has this been going on?"

"I have always been fond of Margaret, sir; but I was not aware of the strength of the attachment until the time of her illness, when I - that is, we - came near to losing her."

"And you, Margaret?"

As Mr. Slocum spoke he instinctively put one arm around Margaret, who had crept closely to his side.

"I don't know when I began to love Richard," said Margaret simply.

"You don't know!"

"Perhaps it was while I was ill; perhaps it was long before that; may be my liking for him commenced as far back as the time he made the cast of my hand. How can I tell, papa? I don't know."

"There appears to be an amazing diffusion of ignorance here!"

Margaret bit her lip, and kept still. Her father was taking it a great deal more seriously than she had expected. A long, awkward silence ensued. Richard broke it at last by remarking uneasily, "Nothing has been or was to be concealed from you. Before going to sleep to-night, Margaret would have told you all I've said to her."

" You should have consulted with me before

saying anything."

"I intended to do so, but my words got away from me. I hope you will overlook it, sir, and not oppose my loving Margaret, though I see as plainly as you do that I am not worthy of her."

"I have not said that. I base my disapproval on entirely different ground. Margaret is too young. A girl of seventeen or eighteen" -

"Nineteen," said Margaret, parenthetically.

"Of nineteen, then, - has no business to bother her head with such matters. Only yesterday she was a child!"

Richard glanced across at Margaret, and endeavored to recall her as she impressed him that first afternoon, when she knocked defiantly at the workshop door to inquire if he wanted any pans and pails; but he was totally unable to reconstruct that crude little figure with the glossy black head, all eyes and beak, like a young hawk's.

"My objection is impersonal," continued Mr. Slocum. "I object to the idea. I wish this had not happened. I might not have disliked it - years hence; I don't say; but I dislike it now."

Richard's face brightened. "It will be years hence in a few years!"

Mr. Slocum replied with a slow, grave smile, "I am not going to be unreasonable in a matter where I find Margaret's happiness concerned; and yours, Richard, I care for that, too; but I'll have no entanglements. You and she are to be good friends, and nothing beyond. I prefer that Margaret should not come to the studio so often; you shall see her whenever you like at our fireside, of an evening. I don't think the conditions hard."

Mr. Slocum had dictated terms, but it was virtually a surrender. Margaret listened to him with her cheek resting against his arm, and a warm light nestled down deep under her eyelids.

Mr. Slocum drew a half-pathetic sigh. "I presume I have not done wisely. Every one bullies me. The Marble Workers' Association ruins my yard for me, and now my daughter is taken off my hands. By the way, Richard," he said, interrupting himself brusquely, and with an air of dismissing the subject, "I forgot what I came for. I've been thinking over Torrini's case, and have concluded that you had better make up his account and discharge him."

"Certainly, sir," replied Richard, with a shadow of dissent in his manner, "if you wish it."

"He causes a deal of trouble in the yard."

"I am afraid he does. Sucha clean workman when he's sober!"

"But he is never sober."

"He has been in a bad way lately, I admit."

"His example demoralizes the men. I can see it day by day."

"I wish he were not so necessary at this moment," observed Richard. "I don't know who else could be trusted with the frieze for the Soldiers' Monument. I'd like to keep him on a week or ten days longer. Suppose I have a plain talk with Torrini?"

"Surely we have enough good hands to stand the loss of one."

"For a special kind of work there is nobody in the yard like Torrini. That is one reason why I want to hold on to him for a while, and there are other reasons."

"Such as what?"

"Well, I think it would not be wholly politic to break with him just now."

"Why not now as well as any time?"

"He has lately been elected secretary of the Association."

"What of that?"

"He has a great deal of influence there."

"If we put him out of the works it seems to me he would lose his importance, if he really has any to speak of."

"You are mistaken if you doubt it. His position gives him a chance to do much mischief, and he would avail himself of it very adroitly, if he had a personal grievance."

"I believe you are actually afraid of the fellow."

Richard smiled. "No, I am not afraid of him, but I don't underrate him. The men look up to Torrini as a sort of leader; he's an effective speaker, and knows very well how to fan a dissatisfaction. Either he or some other disturbing element has recently been at work among the men. There's considerable grumbling in the yard."

"They are always grumbling, aren't they?"

"Most always, but this is more serious than usual; there appears to be a general stir among the trades in the village. I don't understand it clearly. The marble workers have been holding secret meetings."

"They mean business, you think?"

"They mean increased wages, perhaps."

"But we are now paying from five to ten per cent more than any trade in the place. What are they after?"

"So far as I can gather, sir, the finishers and the slab-sawers want an advance, - I don't know how much. Then there's some talk about having the yard closed an hour earlier on Saturdays. All this is merely rumor; but I am sure there is something in it."

"Confound the whole lot! If we can't discharge a drunken hand without raising the pay of all t he rest, we had better turn over the entire business to the Association. But do as you like, Richard. You see how I am bullied, Margaret. He runs everything! Come, dear."

And Mr. Slocum quitted the workshop, taking Margaret with him. Richard remained standing awhile by the table, in a deep study, with his eyes fixed on the floor. He thought of his early days in the sepulchral house in Welch's Court, of his wanderings abroad, his long years of toil since then, and this sudden blissful love that had come to him, and Mr. Slocum's generosity. Then he thought of Torrini, and went down into the yard gently to admonish the man, for Richard' heart that hour was full of kindness for all the world.

XI

In spite of Mr. Slocum's stipulations respecting the frequency of Margaret's visits to the studio, she was free to come and go as she liked. It was easy for him to say, Be good friends, and nothing beyond; but after that day in the workshop it was impossible for Richard and Margaret to be anything but lovers. The hollowness of pretending otherwise was clear even to Mr. Slocum. In the love of a father for a daughter there is always a vague jealousy which refuses to render a coherent explanation of itself. Mr. Slocum did not escape this, but he managed, nevertheless, to accept the inevitable with very fair grace, and presently to confess to himself that the occurrence which had at first taken him aback was the most natural in the world. That Margaret and Richard, thrown together as they had been, should end by falling in love with each other was not a result to justify much surprise. Indeed, there was a special propriety in their doing so. The Shackfords had always been reputable people in the village, - down to Lemuel Shackford, who of course as an old musk-rat. The family attributes of amiability and honesty had skipped him, but they had reappeared in Richard. It was through his foresight and personal energy that the most lucrative branch of the trade had been established. His services entitled him to a future interest in the business, and Mr. Slocum had intended he should have it. Mr. Slocum had not dreamed of

Thomas Bailey Aldrich

throwing in Margaret also; but since that addition had suggested itself, it seemed to him one of the happy features of the arrangement. Richard would thus be doubly identified with the yard, to which, in fact, he had become more necessary than Mr. Slocum himself.

"He has more backbone with the men than I have," acknowledged Mr. Slocum. "He knows how to manage them, and I don't."

As soft as Slocum was a Stillwater proverb. Richard certainly had plenty of backbone; it was his only capital. In Mr. Slocum's estimation it was sufficient capital. But Lemuel Shackford was a very rich man, and Mr. Slocum could not avoid seeing that it would be decent in Richard's only surviving relative if, at this juncture, he were to display a little interest in the young fellow's welfare.

"If he would only offer to advance a few thousand dollars for Richard," said Mr. Slocum, one evening, to Margaret, with whom he had been talking over the future - "the property must all come to him some time, - it would be a vast satisfaction to me to tell the old man that we can get along without any of his ill-gotten gains. He made the bulk of his fortune during the war, you know. The old sea-serpent," continued Mr. Slocum, with hopeless confusion of metaphor, "had a hand in fitting out more than one blockade-runner. They used to talk of a ship that got away from Charleston with a cargo of cotton that netted the share-holders upwards of two hundred thousand dollars. He denies it now, but everybody knows Shackford. He'd betray his country for fifty cents in postage-stamps."

"Oh, papa! you are too hard on him."

In words dropped cursorily from time to time, Margaret imparted to Richard the substance of her father's speech, and it set Richard reflecting. It was not among the probabilities that Lemuel Shackford would advance a dollar to establish Richard, but if he could induce his cousin even to take the matter into consideration, Richard felt that it would be a kind of moral support to him circumstanced as he was. His pride revolted at the idea of coming quite unbacked and disowned, as well as empty-handed, to Mr. Slocum.

For the last twelve months there had been a cessation of ordinary courtesies between the two cousins. They now passed each other on the street without recognition. A year previously Mr. Shackford had fallen ill, and Richard, aware of the inefficient domestic arrangements in Welch's Court, had gone to the house out of sheer pity. The old man was in bed, and weak with fever, but at seeing Richard he managed to raise himself on one elbow.

"Oh, it's you!" he exclaimed, mockingly. "When a rich man is sick the anxious heirs crowd around him; but they're twice as honestly anxious when he is perfectly well."

"I came to see if I could do anything for you!" cried Richard, with a ferocious glare, and in a tone that went curiously with his words, and shook to the foundations his character of Good Samaritan.

"The only thing you can do for me is to go away."

"I'll do that with pleasure," retorted Richard bitterly.

And Richard went, vowing he would never set foot across the threshold again. He could not help having ugly thoughts. Why should all the efforts to bring about a reconciliation and all the forbearance be on his side? Thenceforth the crabbed old man might go to perdition if he wanted to.

And now here was Richard meditating a visit to that same house to beg a favor!

Nothing but his love for Margaret could have dragged him to such a banquet of humble-pie as he knew was spread for his delectation, the morning he passed up the main street of Stillwater and turned into Welch's Court.

As Richard laid his hand on the latch of the gate, Mr. Shackford, who was digging in the front garden, looked up and saw him. Without paying any heed to Richard's amicable salutation, the old man left the shove sticking in the sod, and walked stiffly into the house. At another moment this would have amused Richard, but now he gravely followed his kinsman, and overtook him at the foot of the staircase.

"Cousin Shackford, can you spare me five or ten minutes?"

"Don't know as I can," said Mr. Shackford, with one foot on the lower stair. "Time is valuable. What do you want? You want something."

"Certainly, or I wouldn't think of trespassing on your time."

" Has Slocum thrown you over?" inquired the old man,

turning quickly. A straw which he held between his thin lips helped to give him a singularly alert expression.

"No; Mr. Slocum and I agree the best in the world. I want to talk with you briefly on certain matters; I want to be on decent terms with you, if you will let me."

"Decent terms means money, doesn't it?" asked Mr. Shackford, with a face as wary and lean as a shark's.

"I do wish to talk about money, among other things," returned Richard, whom this brutal directness disconcerted a little, - "money on satisfactory security."

"You can get it anywhere with that."

"So I might, and be asking no favor; but I would rather get it of you, and consider it an obligation."

"I would rather you wouldn't."

"Listen to me a moment."

"Well, I'm listening."

Mr. Shackford stood in an attitude of attention, with his head canted on one side, his eyes fixed on the ceiling, and the straw between his teeth tilted up at an angle of forty degrees.

"I have, as you know, worked my way in the marble yard to the position of general manager," began Richard.

"I didn't know," said Mr. Shackford, "but I understand. You're a sort of head grave-stone maker."

"That is taking a rather gloomy view of it," said Richard, "but no matter. The point is, I hold a responsible position, and I now have a chance to purchase a share in the works."

"Slocum is willing to take you in, eh?"

"Yes."

"Then the concern is hit."

"Hit?"

"Slocum is going into bankruptcy."

"You are wrong there. The yard was never so prosperous; the coming year we shall coin money like a mint."

"You ought to know," said Mr. Shackford, ruminatively. "A thing as good as a mint must be a good thing."

"If I were a partner in the business, I could marry Margaret."

"Who's Margaret?"

"Mr. Slocum's daughter."

"That's where the wind is! Now how much capital would it take to do all that?" inquired Mr. Shackford, with an air of affable speculation.

"Three or four thousand dollars, - perhaps less."

"Well, I wouldn't give three or four cents to have you marry Slocum's daughter. Richard, you can't pull any chestnuts out of the fire with my paw."

Mr. Shackford's interrogation and his more than usual conciliatory manner had lighted a hope which Richard had not brought with him. Its sudden extinguishment was in consequence doubly aggravating.

"Slocum's daughter!" repeated Mr. Shackford. "I'd as soon you would marry Crazy Nan up at the work-house."

The association of Crazy Nan with Margaret sent a red flush into Richard's cheek. He turned angrily towards the door, and then halted, recollecting the resolve he had made not to lose his temper, come what would. If the interview was to end there it had better not have taken place.

"I had no expectation that you would assist me pecuniarily," said Richard, after a moment. "Let us drop the money question; it shouldn't have come up between us. I want you to aid me, not by lending me money, but by giving me your countenance as the head of the family, - by showing a natural interest in my affairs, and seeming disposed to promote them."

"By just seeming?"

"That is really all I desire. If you were to propose to put capital into the concern, Mr. Slocum would refuse it."

"Slocum would refuse it! Why in the devil should he refuse it?"

"Because" - Richard hesitated, finding himself unexpectedly on delicate ground - "because he would not care to enter into business relations with you, under the circumstances."

Mr. Shackford removed the straw from his mouth, and holding it between his thumb and forefinger peered steadily through his half-closed eyelids at Richard.

"I don't understand you."

"The dispute you had long ago, over the piece of meadow land behind the marble yard. Mr. Slocum felt that you bore on him rather heavily in that matter, and has not quite forgiven you for forcing him to rebuild the sheds."

"Bother Slocum and his sheds! I understand him. What I don't understand is *you*. I am to offer Slocum three or four thousand dollars to set you up, and he is to decline to take it. Is that it?"

"That is not it at all," returned Richard. "My statement was this: If you were to propose purchasing a share for me in the works, Mr. Slocum would not entertain the proposition, thinking - as I don't think - that he would mortify you by the refusal of your money."

"The only way Slocum could mortify me would be by getting hold of it. But what are you driving at, anyhow? In one breath you demand several thousand dollars, and in the next breath you tell me that nobody expects it, or wants it, or could be induced to have it on any terms. Perhaps you will inform me what you are here for?"

"That is what you will never discover!" cried Richard. "It is not in you to comprehend the ties of sympathy that ought to hold between two persons situated as we are. In most families this sympathy binds closely at times, - at christenings, or burials, or when some member is about to take an important step in life. Generally speaking, blood is thicker than water; but your blood, cousin Shackford, seems to be a good deal thinner. I came here to consult with you as my sole remaining kinsman, as one authorized by years and position to give me wise counsel and kindly encouragement at the turning point in my fortune. I didn't wish to go among those people like a tramp, with neither kith nor kin to say a word for me. Of course you don't understand that. How should you? A sentiment of that kind is something quite beyond your conception."

Richard's words went into one ear and out the other, without seeming for an instant to arrest Mr. Shackford's attention. The idea of Slocum not accepting money - anybody's money - presented itself to Mr. Shackford in so facetious a light as nearly to throw him into good humor. His foot was on the first step of the staircase, which he now began slowly to mount, giving vent, as he ascended, to a serious of indescribable chuckles. At the top of the landing he halted, and leaned over the rail.

"To think of Slocum refusing, - that's a good one!"

In the midst of his jocularity a sudden thought seemed to strike Mr. Shackford; his features underwent a swift transformation, and as he grasped the rail in front of him with both hands a malicious cunning writhed and squirmed in every wrinkle of his face.

"Sir!" he shrieked, "it was a trap! Slocum would have taken it! If I had been ass enough to make any such offer, he would have jumped at it. What do you and Slocum take me for? You're a pair of rascals!"

Richard staggered back, bewildered and blinded, as if he had received a blow in the eyes.

"No," continued Mr. Shackford, with a gesture of intense contempt, "you are less than rascals. You are fools. A rascal has to have brains!"

"You shameless old man!" cried Richard, as soon as he could get his voice.

To do Mr. Shackford justice, he was thoroughly convinced that Richard had lent himself to a preposterous attempt to obtain money from him. The absence of ordinary shrewdness in the method stamped it at once as belonging to Slocum, of whose mental calibre Mr. Shackford entertained no flattering estimate.

"Slocum!" he muttered, grinding the word between his teeth. "Family ties!" he cried, hurling the words scornfully over the banister as he disappeared into one of the upper chambers.

Richard stood with one hand on the newel-post, white at the lip with rage. For a second he had a wild impulse to spring up the staircase, but, controlling this, he turned and hurried out of the house.

At the gate he brushed roughly against a girl, who halted and stared. It was a strange thing to see Mr. Richard Shackford, who always had a pleasant word for a body, go by in that blind, excited fashion, striking one fist into the palm of the other hand, and talking to his own self! Mary Hennessey watched him until he wheeled out of Welch's Court, and then picking up her basket, which she had rested on the fence, went her way.

Thomas Bailey Aldrich

XII

At the main entrance to the marble works Richard nearly walked over a man who was coming out, intently mopping his forehead with a very dirty calico handkerchief. It was an English stone-dresser named Denyven. Richard did not recognize him at first.

"That you, Denyven! . . . what has happened!"

"I've 'ad a bit of a scrimmage, sir."

"A scrimmage in the yard, in work hours!"

The man nodded.

"With whom?"

"Torrini, sir, - he's awful bad this day."

"Torrini, - it is always Torrini! It seems odd that one man should be everlastingly at the bottom of everything wrong. How did it happen? Give it to me straight, Denyven; I don't want a crooked story. This thing has got to stop in Slocum's Yard."

"The way of it was this, sir: Torrini wasn't at the shop this morning. He 'ad a day off."

"I know."

"But about one o'clock, sir, he come in the yard. He 'ad been at the public 'ouse, sir, and he was hummin'. First he went among the carvers, talking Hitalian to 'em and making 'em laugh, though he was in a precious bad humor hisself. By and by he come over to where me and my mates was, and began chaffin' us, which we didn't mind it, seeing he was 'eavy in the 'ead. He was as clear as a fog 'orn all the same. But when he took to banging the tools on the blocks, I sings out, "Ands off!' and then he fetched me a clip. I was never looking for nothing less than that he'd hit me. I was a smiling at the hinstant."

"He must be drunker than usual."

"Hevidently, sir. I went down between two slabs as soft as you please. When I got on my pins, I was for choking him a bit, but my mates hauled us apart. That's the 'ole of it, sir. They'll tell you the same within."

"Are you hurt, Denyven?"

"Only a bit of a scratch over the heye, sir, - and the nose," and the man began mopping his brow tenderly. "I'd like to 'ave that Hitalian for about ten minutes, some day when he's sober, over yonder on the green."

"I'm afraid he would make the ten minutes seem long to you."

"Well, sir, I'd willingly let him try his 'and."

"How is it, Denyven," said Richard, "that you and sensible workingmen like you, have permitted such a quarrelsome and irresponsible fellow to become a leader in the Association? He's secretary, or something, isn't he?"

"Well, sir, he writes an uncommonly clean fist, and then he's a born horator. He's up to all the parli'mentary dodges. Must 'ave 'ad no end of hexperience in them sort of things on the other side."

"No doubt, - and that accounts for him being over here."

"As for horganizing a meeting, sir" -

"I know. Torrini has a great deal of that kind of ability; perhaps a trifle too much for his own good or anybody else's. There was never any trouble to speak of among the trades in Stillwater till he and two or three others came here with foreign grievances. These men get three times the pay they ever received in their own land, and are treated like human beings for the first time in their lives. But what do they do? They squander a quarter of their week's wages at the tavern, - no rich man could afford to put a fourth of his income into drink, - and make windy speeches at the Union. I don't say all of them, but too many of them. The other night, I understand, Torrini compared Mr. Slocum to Nero, - Mr. Slocum, the fairest and gentlest man that ever breathed! What rubbish!"

"It wasn't just that way, sir. His words was, and I 'eard him, - 'from Nero down to Slocum.'"

"It amounts to the same thing, and is enough to make one laugh, if he didn't make one want to swear. I hear that that was a very lively meeting the other night.

What was that nonsense about 'the privileged class'?"

"Well, there is a privileged class in the States."

"So there is, but it's a large class, Denyven. Every soul of us has the privilege of bettering out condition if we have the brain and the industry to do it. Energy and intelligence come to the front, and have the right to be there. A skillful workman gets double the pay of a bungler, and deserves it. Of course there will always be rich and poor, and sick and sound, and I don't see how that can be changed. But no door is shut against ability, black or white. Before the year 2400 we shall have a chrome-yellow president and a black-and-tan secretary of the treasury. But, seriously, Denyven, whoever talks about privileged classes here does it to make mischief. There are certain small politicians who reap their harvest in times of public confusion, just as pickpockets do. Nobody can play the tyrant or the bully in this country, - not even a workingman. Here's the Association dead against an employer who, two years ago, ran his yard full-handed for a twelvemonth at a loss, rather than shut down, as every other mill and factory in Stillwater did. For years and years the Association has prevented this employer from training more than two apprentices annually. The result is, eighty hands find work, instead of a hundred and eighty. Now, that can't last."

"It keeps wages fixed in Stillwater, sir."

"It keeps out a hundred workmen. It sends away capital."

"Torrini says, sir" -

"Steer clear of Torrini and what he says. He's a dangerous fellow - for his friends. It is handsome in you, Denyven, to speak up for him - with that eye of yours."

"Oh, I don't love the man, when it comes to that; but there's no denying he's right smart," replied Denyven, who occasionally marred his vernacular with Americanisms. "The Association couldn't do without him."

"But Slocum's Yard can," said Richard, irritated to observe the influence Torrini exerted on even such men as Denyven.

"That's between you and him, sir, of course, but" -

"But what?"

"Well, isr, I can't say hexactly; but if I was you I would bide a bit."

"No, I think Torrini's time has come."

"I don't make bold to advise you, sir. I merely throws out the hobservation."

With that Denyven departed to apply to his bruises such herbs and simples as a long experience had taught him to be efficacious.

He had gone only a few rods, however, when it occurred to him that there were probabilities of a stormy scene in the yard; so he turned on his tracks, and followed Richard Shackford.

Torrini was a Neapolitan, who had come to the country seven or eight years before. He was a man above the average intelligence of his class; a marble worker by trade, but he had been a fisherman, a mountain guide among the Abruzzi, a soldier in the papal guard, and what not, and had contrived to pick up two or three languages, among the rest English, which he spoke with purity. His lingual gift was one of his misfortunes.

Among the exotics in Stillwater, which even boasted a featureless Celestial, who had unobtrusively extinguished himself with a stove-pipe hat, Torrini was the only figure that approached picturesqueness. With his swarthy complexion and large, indolent eyes, in which a southern ferocity slept lightly, he seemed to Richard a piece out of his own foreign experience. To him Torrini was the crystallization of Italy, or so much of that Italy as Richard had caught a glimpse of at Genoa. To the town-folks Torrini perhaps vaguely suggested hand-organs and eleemosynary pennies; but Richard never looked at the straight-limbed, handsome fellow without recalling the Phrygian-capped sailors of the Mediterranean. On this account, and for other reasons, Richard had taken a great fancy to the man. Torrini had worked in the ornamental department from the first, and was a rapid and expert carver when he chose. He had carried himself steadily enough in the beginning, but in these later days, as Mr. Slocum had stated, he was scarcely ever sober. Richard had stood between him and his discharge on several occasions, partly because he was so skillful a workman, and partly through pity for his wife and children, who were unable to speak a word of English. But Torrini's influence on the men in the yard, - especially on the younger hands, who needed quite other influences, - and his intemperate speeches at the trades-union, where he had recently gained a kind of ascendancy by his daring, were producing the worst effects.

At another hour Richard might have been inclined to condone this last offense, as he had condoned others; but when he parted from Denyven, Richard's heart was still hot with his cousin's insult. As he turned into the yard, not with his usual swinging gait, but with a quick, wide step, there was an unpleasant dilation about young Shackford's nostrils.

Torrini was seated on a block of granite in front of the upper sheds, flourishing a small chisel in one hand and addressing the men, a number of whom had stopped work to listen to him. At sight of Richard they made a show of handling their tools, but it was so clear something grave was going to happen that the pretense fell through. They remained motionless, resting on their mallets, with their eyes turned towards Richard. Torrini followed the general glance, and pause din his harangue.

"Talk of the devil!" he muttered, and then, apparently continuing the thread of his discourse, broke into a strain of noisy declamation.

Richard walked up to him quietly.

"Torrini," he said, "you can't be allowed to speak here, you know."

"I can speak where I like," replied Torrini gravely. He was drunk, but the intoxication was not in his tongue. His head, as Denyven had asserted, was as clear as a fog-horn.

"When you are sober, you can come to the desk and get your pay and your kit. You are discharged from the yard."

Richard was standing within two paces of the man, who looked up with an uncertain smile, as if he had not quite taken in the sense of the words. Then, suddenly straightening himself, he exclaimed, -

"Slocum don't dare do it!"

"But I do."

"You!"

"When I do a thing Mr. Slocum backs me."

"But who backs Slocum, - the Association, may be?"

"Certainly the Association ought to. I want you to leave the yard now."

"He backs Slocum," said Torrini, settling himself on the block again, "and Slocum backs down," at which there was a laugh among the men.

Richard made a step forward.

"Hands off!" cried a voice from under the sheds.

"Who said that?" demanded Richard, wheeling around. No one answered, but Richard had recognized Durgin's voice. "Torrini, if you don't quit the yard in two minutes by the clock yonder, I shall put you out by the neck. Do you understand?"

Thomas Bailey Aldrich

Torrini glared about him confusedly for a moment, and broke into voluble Italian; then, without a warning gesture, sprung to his feet and struck at Richard. A straight red line, running vertically the length of his cheek, showed where the chisel had grazed him. The shops were instantly in a tumult, the men dropping their tools and stumbling over the blocks, with cries of "Keep them apart!" "Shame on you!" "Look out, Mr. Shackford!"

"Is it mad ye are, Torrany!" cried Michael Hennessey, hurrying from the saw-bench. Durgin held him back by the shoulders.

"Let them alone," said Durgin.

The flat steel flashed again in the sunlight, but fell harmlessly, and before the blow could be repeated, Richard had knitted his fingers in Torrini's neckerchief and twisted it so tightly that the man gasped. Holding him by this, Richard dragged Torrini across the yard, and let him drop on the sidewalk outside the gate, where he lay in a heap, inert.

"That was nate," said Michael Hennessey, sententiously.

Richard stood leaning on the gate-post to recover he breath. His face was colorless, and the crimson line defined itself sharply against the pallor; but the rage was dead within him. It had been one of his own kind of rages, - like lightning out of a blue sky. As he stood there a smile was slowly gathering on his lip.

A score or two of the men had followed him, and now lounged in a half-circle a few paces in the rear. When

Richard was aware of their presence, the glow came into his eyes again.

"Who ordered you to knock off work?"

"That was a foul blow of Torrini's, sir," said Stevens, stepping forward, "and I for one come to see fair play."

"Give us your 'and, mate!" cried Denyven; "there's a pair of us."

"Thanks," said Richard, softening at once, "but there's no need. Every man can go to his job. Denyven may stay, if he likes."

The men lingered a moment, irresolute, and returned to the sheds in silence.

Presently Torrini stretched out one leg, then the other, and slowly rose to his feet, giving a stupid glance at his empty hands as he did so.

"Here's your tool," said Richard, stirring the chisel with the toe of his boot, "if that's what you're looking for."

Torrini advanced a step as if to pick it up, then appeared to alter his mind, hesitated perhaps a dozen seconds, and turning abruptly on his heel walked down the street without a stagger.

"I think his legs is shut off from the rest of his body by water-tight compartments," remarked Denyven, regarding Torrini's steady gait with mingled amusement and envy. "Are you hurt, sir?"

"Only a bit of a scratch of the heye," replied Richard, with a laugh.

"As I hobserved just now to Mr. Stevens, sir, there's a pair of us!"

XIII

After a turn through the shops to assure himself that order was restored, Richard withdrew in the direction of his studio. Margaret was standing at the head of the stairs, half hidden by the scarlet creeper which draped that end of the veranda.

"What are you doing there?" said Richard looking up with a bright smile.

"Oh, Richard, I saw it all!"

"You didn't see anything worth having white cheeks about."

"But he struck you . . . with the knife, did he not?" said Margaret, clinging to his arm anxiously.

"He didn't have a knife, dear; only a small chisel, which couldn't hurt any one. See for yourself; it is merely a cat-scratch."

Margaret satisfied herself that it was nothing more; but she nevertheless insisted on leading Richard into the workshop, and soothing the slight inflammation with her handkerchief dipped in arnica and water. The elusive faint fragrance of Margaret's hair as she busied herself about him would of itself have consoled

Richard for a deep wound. All this pretty solicitude and ministration was new and sweet to him, and when the arnica turned out to be cologne, and scorched his cheek, Margaret's remorse was so delicious that Richard half wished the mixture had been aquafortia.

"You shouldn't have been looking into the yard," he said. "If I had known that you were watching us it would have distracted me. When I am thinking of you I cannot think of anything else, and I had need of my wits for a moment."

"I happened to be on the veranda, and was too frightened to go away. Why did you quarrel?"

In giving Margaret an account of the matter, Richard refrained from any mention of his humiliating visit to Welch's Court that morning. He could neither speak of it nor reflect upon it with composure. The cloud which shadowed his features from time to time was attributed by Margaret to the affair in the yard.

"But this is the end of it, is it not?" she asked, with troubled eyes. "You will not have any further words with him?"

"You needn't worry. If Torrini had not been drinking he would never have lifted his hand against me. When he comes out of his present state, he will be heartily ashamed of himself. His tongue is the only malicious part of him. If he hadn't a taste for drink and oratory, - if he was not 'a born horator,' as Denyven calls him, - he would do well enough."

"No, Richard, he's a dreadful man. I shall never forget his face, - it was some wild animal's. And you,

Richard," added Margaret softly, "it grieved me to see you look like that."

"I was wolfish for a moment, I suppose. Things had gone wrong generally. But if you are going to scold me, Margaret, I would rather have some more - arnica."

"I am not going to scold; but while you stood there, so white and terrible, - so unlike yourself, - I felt that I did not know you, Richard. Of course you had to defend yourself when the man attacked you, but I thought for an instant you would kill him."

"Not I," said Richard uneasily, dreading anything like a rebuke from Margaret. "I am mortified that I gave up to my anger. There was no occasion."

"If an intoxicated person were to wander into the yard, papa would send for a constable, and have the person removed."

"Your father is an elderly man," returned Richard, not relishing this oblique criticism of his own simpler method. "What would be proper in his case would be considered cowardly in mine. It was my duty to discharge the fellow, and not let him dispute my authority. I ought to have been cooler, of course. But I should have lost caste and influence with the men if I had shown the least personal fear of Torrini, - if, for example, I had summoned somebody else to do what I didn't dare do myself. I was brought up in the yard, remember, and to a certain extent I have to submit to being weighed in the yard's own scales."

"But a thing cannot be weighed in a scale incapable of

containing it," answered Margaret. "The judgment of these rough, uninstruicted men is too narrow for such as you. They quarrel and fight among themselves, and have their ideas of daring; but there is a higher sort of bravery, the bravery of self-control, which I fancy they do not understand very well; so their opinion of it is not worth considering. However, you know better than I."

"No, I do not," said Richard. "Your instinct is finer than my reason. But you *are* scolding me, Margaret."

"No, I am loving you," she said softly. "How can I do that more faithfully than by being dissatisfied with anything but the best in you?"

"I wasn't at my best a while ago?"

"No, Richard."

"I can never hope to be worthy of you."

But Margaret protested against that. Having forced him to look at his action through her eyes, she outdid him in humility, and then the conversation drifted off into half-breathed nothings, which, though they were satisfactory enough for these two, would have made a third person yawn.

The occurrence at Slocum's Yard was hotly discussed that night at the Stillwater hotel. Discussions in that long, low bar-room, where the latest village scandal always came to receive the finishing gloss, were apt to be hot. In their criticism of outside men and measures, as well as in their mutual vivisections, there was an unflinching directness among Mr. Snelling's guests which is not to be found in more artificial grades of society. The popular verdict on young Shackford's conduct was as might not have been predicted, strongly in his favor. He had displayed pluck, and pluck of the tougher fibre was a quality held in so high esteem in Stillwater that any manifestation of it commanded respect. And young Shackford had shown a great deal; he had made short work of the most formidable man in the yard, and given the rest to understand that he was not to be tampered with. This had taken many by surprise, for hitherto an imperturbable amiability had been the leading characteristic of Slocum's manager.

"I didn't think he had it in him," declared Dexter.

"Well, ye might," replied Michael Hennessey. "Look at the lad's eye, and the muscles of him. He stands on his own two legs like a monumint, so he does."

"Never saw a monument with two legs, Mike."

"Didn't ye? Wait till ye're layin' at the foot of one. But ye'll wait many a day, me boy. Ye'll be lucky if ye're supploid with a head-stone made out of a dale-board."

"Couldn't get a wooden head-stone short of Ireland, Mike." Retorted Dexter, with a laugh. "You'd have to import it."

"An' so I will; but it won't be got over in time, if ye go on interruptin' gintlemen when they're discoorsin'. What was I sayin', any way, when the blackguard chipped in?" continued Mr. Hennessey, appealing to the company, as he emptied the ashes from his pipe by knocking the bowl in the side of his chair.

"You was talking of Dick Shackford's muscle," said Durgin, "and you never talked wider of the mark. It doesn't take much muscle, or much courage either, to knock a man about when he's in liquor. The two wasn't fairly matched."

"You are right there, Durgin," said Stevens, laying down his newspaper. "They weren't fairly matched. Both men have the same pounds and inches, but Torrini had a weapon and that mad strength that comes to some folks with drink. If Shackford hadn't made a neat twist on the neckerchief, he wouldn't have got off with a scratch."

"Shackford had no call to lay hands on him."

"There you are wrong, Durgin," replied Stevens. "Torrini had no call in the yard; he was making a nuisance of himself. Shackford spoke to him, and told him to go, and when he didn't go Shackford put him out; and he put him out handsomely, - 'with neatness and dispatch,' as Slocum's prospectuses has it."

"He was right all the time," said Piggott. "He didn't strike Torrini before or after he was down, and stood at the gate like a gentleman, ready to give Torrini his chance if he wanted it."

"Torrini didn't want it," observed Jemmy Willson. "Ther' isn't nothing mean about Torrini."

"But he 'ad a dozen minds about coming back," said Denyven.

"We ought to have got him out of the place quietly," said Jeff Stavers; "that was our end of the mistake. He is not a bad fellow, but he shouldn't drink."

"He was crazy to come to the yard."

"When a man 'as a day off," observed Denyven, "and the beer isn't narsty, he 'ad better stick to the public 'ouse."

"Oh, you!" exclaimed Durgin. "Your opinion don't weigh. You took a black eye of him."

"Yes, I took a black heye, - and I can give one, in a hemergency. Yes, I gives and takes."

"That's where we differ," returned Durgin. "I do a more genteel business; I give, and don't take."

"Unless you're uncommon careful," said Denyven, pulling away at his pipe, "you'll find yourself some day henlarging your business."

Durgin pushed back his stool.

"Gentlemen! gentlemen!" interposed Mr. Snelling, appearing from beind the bar with a lemon-squeezer in his hand, "we'll have no black eyes here that wasn't born so. I am partial to them myself when nature gives them; and I propose the health of Miss Molly Hennessey," with a sly glance at Durgin, who colored, "to be drank at the expense of the house. Name your taps, gentlemen."

"Snelling, me boy, ye'd wint the bird from the bush with yer beguilin' ways. Ye've brought proud tears to the eyes of an aged parent, and I'll take a sup out of that high-showldered bottle which you kape under the counter for the gentle-folk in the other room."

A general laugh greeted Mr. Hennessey's selection, and peace was restored; but the majority of those present were workmen from Slocum's, and the event of the afternoon remained the uppermost theme.

"Shackford is a different build from Slocum," said Piggott.

"I guess the yard will find that out when he gets to be proprietor," rejoined Durgin, clicking his spoon against the empty glass to attract Snelling's attention.

"Going to be proprietor, is he?"

"Some day or other," answered Durgin. "First he'll step into the business, and then into the family. He's had his eye on Slocum's girl these four or five years. Got a cast of her fist up in his workshop. Leave Dick Shackford alone for lining his nest and making it soft all round."

"Why shouldn't he?" asked Stevens. "He deserves a good girl, and there's none better. If sickness or any sort of trouble comes to a poor man's door, she's never far off with her kind words and them things the rich have when they are laid up."

"Oh, the girl is well enough."

"You couldn't say less. Before your mother died," - Mrs. Durgin had died the previous autumn, - "I see that angil going to your house many a day with a little basket of comforts tucked under her wing. But she's too good to be praised in such a place as this," added Stevens. After a pause he inquired, "What makes you down on Shackford? He has always been a friend to you."

"One of those friends who walk over your head," replied Durgin. "I was in the yard two years before him, and see where he is."

"Lord love you," said Stevens, leaning back in his chair and contemplating Durgin thoughtfully, "there is marble and marble; some is Carrara marble, and some isn't. The fine grain takes a polish you can't get on to the other."

"Of course, he is statuary marble, and I'm full of seams and feldspar."

"You are like the most of us, - not the kind that can be worked up into anything very ornamental."

"Thank you for nothing," said Durgin, turning away. "I came from as good a quarry as ever Dick Shackford. Where's Torrini to-night?"

"Nobody has seen him since the difficulty," said Dexter, "except Peters. Torrini sent for him after supper."

As Dexter spoke, the door opened and Peters entered. He went directly to the group composed chiefly of Slocum's men, and without making any remark began to distribute among them certain small blue tickets, which they pocketed in silence. Glancing carelessly at his piece of card-board, Durgin said to Peters, -

"Then it's decided?"

Peters nodded.

"How's Torrini?"

"He's all right."

"What does he say?"

"Nothing in perticular," responded Peters, "and nothing at all about his little skylark with Shackford."

"He's a cool one!" exclaimed Durgin.

Though the slips of blue pasteboard had been delivered and accepted without comment, it was known in a second through the bar-room that a special meeting had been convened for the next night by the officers of the Marble Workers' Association.

XIV

On the third morning after Torrini's expulsion from the yard, Mr. Slocum walked into the studio with a printed slip in his hand. A similar slip lay crumpled under a work-bench, where Richard had tossed it. Mr. Slocum's kindly visage was full of trouble and perplexity as he raised his eyes from the paper, which he had been re-reading on the way up-stairs.

"Look at that!"

"Yes," remarked Richard, "I have been honored with one of those documents."

"What does it mean?"

"It means business."

The paper in question contained a series of resolutions unanimously adopted at a meeting of the Marble Workers' Association of Stillwater, held in Grimsey's Hall the previous night. Dropping the preamble, these resolutions, which were neatly printed with a type-writing machine on a half letter sheet, ran as follows: -

Resolved, That on and after the First of June proximo, the pay of carvers in Slocum's Marble Yard shall be $2.75 per day, instead of $2.50 as heretofore.

Resolved, That on and after the same date, the rubbers and polishers shall have $2.00 per day, instead of $1.75 as heretofore.

Resolved, That on and after the same date the millmen are to have $2.00 per day, instead of $1.75 as heretofore.

Resolved, That during the months of June, July, and August the shops shall knock off work on Saturdays at five P.M., instead of at six P.M.

Resolved, That a printed copy of these Resolutions be laid before the Proprietor of Slocum's Marble Yard, and that his immediate attention to them be respectfully requested. *Per order of Committee M. W. A.*

"Torrini is at the bottom of that," said Mr. Slocum.

"I hardly think so. This arrangement, as I told you the other day before I had the trouble with him, has been in contemplation several weeks. Undoubtedly Torrini used his influence to hasten the movement already planned. The Association has too much shrewdness to espouse the quarrel of an individual."

"What are we to do?"

"If you are in the same mind you were when we talked over the possibility of an unreasonable demand like this, there is only one thing to do."

"Fight it?"

"Fight it."

"I have been resolute, and all that sort of thing, in times past," observed Mr. Slocum, glancing out of the tail of his eye at Richard, "and have always come off second best. The Association has drawn up most of my rules for me, and had its own way generally."

"Since my time you have never been in so strong a position to make a stand. We have got all the larger contracts out of the way. Foreseeing what was likely to come, I have lately fought shy of taking new ones. Here are heavy orders from Rafter & Son, the Builders' Company, and others. We must decline them by to-night's mail."

"Is it really necessary?" asked Mr. Slocum, knitting his forehead into what would have been a scowl if his mild pinkish eyebrows had permitted it.

"I think so."

"I hate to do that."

"Then we are at the mercy of the Association."

"If we do not come to their terms, you seriously believe they will strike?"

"I do," replied Richard, "and we should be in a pretty fix."

"But these demands are ridiculous."

"The men are not aware of our situation; they imagine we have a lot of important jobs on hand, as usual at this season. Formerly the foreman of a shop had access to the order-book, but for the last year or two I have kept it in the safe here. The other day Dexter came to me and wanted to see what work was set down ahead in the blotter; but I had an inspiration and didn't let him post himself."

"Is not some kind of compromise possible?" suggested Mr. Slocum, looking over the slip again. "Now this fourth clause, about closing the yard an hour early on Saturdays, I don't strongly object to that, though with eighty hands it means, every week, eighty hours' work which the yard pays for and doesn't get."

"I should advise granting that request. Such concessions are never wasted. But, Mr. Slocum, this is not going to satisfy them. They have thrown in one reasonable demand merely to flavor the rest. I happen to know that they are determined to stand by their programme to the last letter."

"You know that?"

"I have a friend at court. Of course this is not to be breathed, but Denyven, without being at all false to his comrades, talks freely with me. He says they are resolved not to give an inch."

"Then we will close the works."

"That is what I wanted you to say, sir!" cried Richard.

"With this new scale of prices and plenty of work, we might probably come out a little ahead the next six months; but it wouldn't pay for the trouble and the capital invested. Then when trade slackened, we should be running at a loss, and there'd be another wrangle over a reduction. We had better lie idle."

"Stick to that, sir, and may be it will not be necessary."

"But if they strike" -

"They won't all strike. At least," added Richard, "I hope not. I have indirectly sounded several of the older hands, and they have half promised to hold on; only half promised, for every man of them at heart fears the trades-union more than No-bread - until No-bread comes."

"Whom have you spoken with?"

"Lumley, Giles, Peterson, and some others, - your pensioners, I call them."

"Yes, they were in the yard in my father's time; they have not been worth their salt these ten years. When the business was turned over to me I didn't discharge any old hand who had given his best days to the yard. Somehow I couldn't throw away the squeezed lemons. An employer owes a good workman something beyond the wages paid."

"And a workman owes a good employer something beyond the work done. You stood by these men after they outlived their usefulness, and if they do not stand by you now, they're a shabby set."

"I fancy they will, Richard."

"I think they had better, and I wish they would. We have enough odds and ends to keep them busy awhile, and I shouldn't like to have the clinking of chisels die out altogether under the old sheds."

"Nor I," returned Mr. Slocum, with a touch of sadness in his intonation. "It has grown to be a kind of music to me," and he paused to listen to the sounds of ringing steel that floated up from the workshop.

"Whatever happens, that music shall not cease in the yard except on Sundays, if I have to take the mallet and go at a slab all alone."

"Slocum's Yard with a single workman in it would be a pleasing spectacle," said Mr. Slocum, smiling ruefully.

"It wouldn't be a bad time for *that* workman to strike," returned Richard with a laugh.

"He could dictate his own terms," returned Mr. Slocum, soberly. "Well, I suppose you cannot help thinking about Margaret; but don't think of her now. Tell me what answer you propose to give the Association, - how you mean to put it; for I leave the matter wholly to you. I shall have no hand in it, further than to indorse your action."

"To-morrow, then," said Richard, "for it is no use to hurry up a crisis, I shall go to the workshops and inform them that their request for short hours on Saturdays is granted, but that the other changes they suggest are not to be considered. There will never be a better opportunity, Mr. Slocum, to settle another question which has been allowed to run too long."

"What's that?"

"The apprentice question."

"Would it be wise to touch on that at present?"

"While we are straightening out matters and putting things on a solid basis, it seems to me essential to settle that. There was never a greater imposition, or one more short-sighted, than this rule which prevents the training of sufficient workmen. The trades-union will discover their error some day when they have succeeded in forcing manufacturers to import skilled labor by the wholesale. I would like to tell the Marble Workers' Association that Slocum's Yard has resolved to employ as many apprentices each year as there is room for."

"I wouldn't dare risk it!"

"It will have to be done, sooner or later. It would be a capital flank movement now. They have laid themselves open to an attack on that quarter."

"I might as well close the gates for good and all."

"So you will, if it comes to that. You can afford to close the gates, and they can't afford to have you. In a week they'd be back, asking you to open them. Then you could have your pick of the live hands, and drop the dead wood. If Giles or Peterson or Lumley or any of those desert us, they are not to be let on again. I hope you will promise me that, sir."

"If the occasion offers, you shall reorganize the shops in your own way. I haven't the nerve for this kind of business, though I have seen a great deal of it in the villages, first and last. Strikes are terrible mistakes. Even when they succeed, what pays for the lost time and the money squandered over the tavern-bar? What makes up for the days or weeks when the fire was out on the hearth and the children had no bread? That is what happens, you know."

"There is no remedy for such calamities," Richard answered. "Yet I can imagine occasions when it would be better to let the fire go out and the children want for bread."

"You are not advocating strikes!" exclaimed Mr. Slocum.

"Why not?"

"I thought you were for fighting them."

"So I am, in this instance; but the question has two sides. Every man has the right to set a price on his own labor, and to refuse to work for less; the wisdom of it is another matter. He puts himself in the wrong only when he menaces the person or the property of the man who has an equal right not to employ him. That is the blunder strikers usually make in the end, and one by which they lose public sympathy even when they are fighting an injustice. Now, sometimes it *is* an injustice that is being fought, and then it is right to fight it with the only weapon a poor man has to wield against a power which possesses a hundred weapons, - and that's a strike. For example, the smelters and casters in the Miantowona Iron Works are meanly underpaid."

"What, have they struck?"

"There's a general strike threatened in the village; foundry-men, spinners, and all."

"So much the worse for everybody! I did not suppose it was as bad as that. What has become of Torrini?"

"The day after he left us he was taken on as forgeman

at Dana's."

"I am glad Dana has got him!"

"At the meeting, last night, Torrini gave in his resignation as secretary of the Association; being no longer a marble worker, he was not qualified to serve."

"We unhorsed him, then?"

"Rather. I am half sorry, too."

"Richard," said Mr. Slocum, halting in one of his nervous walks up and down the room, "you are the oddest composition of hardness and softness I ever saw."

"Am I?"

"One moment you stand braced like a lion to fight the whole yard, and the next moment you are pitying a miscreant who would have laid your head open without the slightest compunction."

"Oh, I forgive him," said Richard. "I was a trifle hasty myself. Margaret thinks so too."

"Much Margaret knows about it!"

"I was inconsiderate, to say the least. When a man picks up a tool by the wrong end he must expect to get cut."

"You didn't have a choice."

"I shouldn't have touched Torrini. After discharging

Thomas Bailey Aldrich

him and finding him disposed to resist my order to leave the yard, I ought to have called in a constable. Usually it is very hard to anger me; but three or four times in my life I have been carried away by a devil of a temper which I couldn't control, it seized me so unawares. That was one of the times."

The mallets and chisels were executing a blithe staccato movement in the yard below, and making the sparks dance. No one walking among the diligent gangs, and observing the placid faces of the men as they bent over their tasks, would have suspected that they were awaiting the word that meant bread and meat and home to them.

As Richard passed through the shops, dropping a word to a workman here and there, the man addressed looked up cheerfully and made a furtive dab at the brown paper cap, and Richard returned the salute smilingly; but he was sad within. "The foolish fellows," he said to himself, "they are throwing away a full loaf and are likely to get none at all." Giles and two or three of the ancients were squaring a block of marble under a shelter by themselves. Richard made it a point to cross over and speak to them. In past days he had not been exacting with these old boys, and they always had a welcome for him.

Slocum's Yard seldom presented a serener air of contented industry than it wore that morning; but in spite of all this smooth outside it was a foregone conclusion with most of the men that Slocum, with Shackford behind him, would never submit to the new scale of wages. There were a few who had protested against these resolutions and still disapproved of them, but were forced to go with the Association, which had really been dragged into the current by the other trades.

The Dana Mills and the Miantowona Iron Works were paying lighter wages than similar establishments nearer the great city. The managers contended that they were paying as high if not higher rates, taking into consideration the cheaper cost of living in Stillwater. "But you get city prices for your wares," retorted the union; "you don't pay city rents, and you shall pay city wages." Meetings were held at Grimsey's Hall and the subject was canvassed, at first calmly and then stormily. Among the molders, and possibly the sheet-iron workers, there was cause for dissatisfaction; but the dissatisfaction spread to where no grievance existed; it seized upon the spinners, and finally upon the marble workers. Torrini fanned the flame there. Taking for his text the rentage question, he argued that Slocum was well able to give a trifle more for labor than his city competitors. "The annual rent of a yard like Slocum's would be four thousand or five thousand dollars in the city. It doesn't cost Slocum two hundred dollars. It is no more than just that the laborer should have a share - he only asks a beggarly share - of the prosperity which he has helped to build up." This was specious and taking. Then there came down from the great city a glib person disguised as The Workingman's Friend, - no workingman himself, mind you, but a ghoul that lives upon subscriptions and sucks the senses out of innocent human beings, - who managed to set the place by the ears. The result of all which was that one May morning every shop, mill, and factory in Stillwater was served with a notice from the trades-union, and a general strike threatened.

But our business at present is exclusively with Slocum's Yard.

XV

"Since we are in for it," said Mr. Slocum the next
morning, "put the case to them squarely."

Mr. Slocum's vertebræ had stiffened over night.

"Leave that to me, sir," Richard replied. "I have been
shaping out in my mind a little speech which I flatter
myself will cover the points. They have brought this
thing upon themselves, and we are about to have the
clearest of understandings. I never saw the men
quieter."

"I don't altogether admire that. It looks as if they hadn't
any doubt as to the issue."

"The clearest-headed have no doubt; they know as well
as you and I do the flimsiness of those resolutions. But
the thick heads are in a fog. Every man naturally likes
his pay increased; if a simple fellow is told five or six
hundred times that his wages ought to be raised, the
idea is so agreeable and insidious that by and by he
begins to believe himself grossly underpaid, though he
may be getting twice what he is worth. He doesn't
reason about it; that's the last thing he'll do for you. In
this mood he lets himself be flown away by the breath
of some loud-mouthed demagogue, who has no interest
in the matter beyond hearing his own talk and passing

round the hat after the meeting is over. That is what has happened to our folks below. But they *are* behaving handsomely."

"Yes, and I don't like it."

Since seven o'clock the most unimpeachable decorum had reigned in the workshops. It was now nine, and this brief dialogue had occurred between Mr. Slocum and Richard on the veranda, just as the latter was on the point of descending into the yard to have his talk with the men.

The workshops - or rather the shed in which the workshops were, for it was one low structure eighteen or twenty feet wide and open on the west side - ran the length of the yard, and with the short extension at the southerly end formed the letter L. There were no partitions, an imaginary line separating the different gangs of workers. A person standing at the head of the building could make himself heard more or less distinctly in the remotest part.

The grating lisp of the wet saws eating their way into the marble bowlder, and the irregular quick taps of the seventy or eighty mallets were not suspended as Richard took his stand beside a tall funereal urn at the head of the principal workshop. After a second's faltering he rapped smartly on the lip of the ukrn with the key of his studio-door.

Instantly every arm appeared paralyzed, and the men stood motionless, with the tools in their hands.

Richard began in a clear but not loud voice, though it seemed to ring on the sudden silence: -

"Mr. Slocum has asked me to say a few words to you, this morning, about those resolutions, and one or two other matters that have occurred to him in this connection. I am no speech-maker; I never learned that trade" -

"Never learned any trade," muttered Durgin, inaudibly.

- "but I think I can manage some plain, honest talk, for straight-forward men."

Richard's exordium was listened to with painful attention.

"In the first place," he continued, "I want to remind you, especially the newer men, that Slocum's Yard has always given steady work and prompt pay to Stillwater hands. No hand has ever been turned off without sufficient cause, or kept on through mere favoritism. Favors have been shown, but they have been shown to all alike. If anything has gone crooked, it has been straightened out as soon as Mr. Slocum knew of it. That has been the course of the yard in the past, and the Proprietor doesn't want you to run away with the idea that that course is going to be changed. One change, for the time being, is going to be made at our own suggestion. From now, until the 1st of September, this yard will close gates on Saturdays at five P.M. instead of six P.M."

Several voices cried, "Good for Slocum!" "Where's Slocum?" "Why don't Slocum speak for himself?" cried one voice.

"It is Mr. Slocum's habit," answered Richard, "to give his directions to me, I give them to the foremen, and the foremen to the shops. Mr. Slocum follows that custom on this occasion. With regard to the new scale of wages which the Association has submitted to him, the Proprietor refuses to accept it, or any modification of it."

A low murmur ran through the workshops.

"What's a modificashun, sir?" asked Jemmy Willson, stepping forward, and scratching his left ear diffidently.

"A modification," replied Richard, considerably embarrassed to give an instant definition, "is a - a" -

"A splitting of the difference, by -!" shouted somebody in the third shop.

"Thank you," said Richard, glancing in the direction of his impromptu Webster's Unabridged. "Mr. Slocum does not propose to split the difference. The wages in every department are to be just what they are, - neither more nor less. If anybody wishes to make a remark," he added, observing a restlessness in several of the men, "I beg he will hold on until I get through. I shall not detain you much longer, as the parson says before he has reached the middle of his sermon.

"What I say now, I was charged to make particularly clear to you. It is this: In future Mr. Slocum intends to run Slocum's Yard himself. Neither you, nor I, nor the Association will be allowed to run it for him. [Sensation.] Until now the Association has tied him down to two apprentices a year. From this hour, out, Mr. Slocum will take on, not two, or twenty, but two hundred apprentices if the business warrants it."

The words were not clearly off Richard's lips when the foreman of the shop in which he was speaking picked up a couple of small drills, and knocked them together with a sharp click. In an instant the men laid aside their aprons, bundled up their tools, and marched out of the shed two by two, in dead silence. That same click was repeated almost simultaneously in the second shop, and the same evolution took place. Then click, click, click! went the drills, sounding fainter and fainter in the distant departments; and in less than three minutes there was not a soul left in Slocum's Yard except the Orator of the Day.

Richard had anticipated some demonstration, either noisy or violent, perhaps both; but this solemn, orderly desertion dashed him.

He stepped into the middle of the yard, and glancing up beheld Margaret and Mr. Slocum standing on the veranda. Even at that distance he could perceive the pallor on one face, and the consternation written all over the other.

Hanging his head with sadness, Richard crossed the yard, which gave out mournful echoes to his footfalls, and swung to the large gate, nearly catching old Giles by the heel as he did so. Looking through the slats, he saw Lumley and Peterson hobbling arm in arm down the street, - after more than twenty-five years of kindly treatment.

"Move number one," said Richard, lifting the heavy cross-piece into its place and fastening it with a wooden pin. "Now I must go and prop up Mr. Slocum."

XVI

There is no solitude which comes so near being tangible as that of a vast empty workshop, crowded a moment since. The busy, intense life that has gone from it mysteriously leaves behind enough of itself to make the stillness poignant. One might imagine the invisible ghost of doomed Toil wandering from bench to bench, and noiselessly fingering the dropped tools, still warm from the workman's palm. Perhaps this impalpable presence is the artisan's anxious thought, stolen back to brood over the uncompleted task.

Though Mr. Slocum had spoken lightly of Slocum's Yard with only one workman in it, when he came to contemplate the actual fact he was struck by the pathos of it, and the resolution with which he awoke that morning began to desert him.

"The worst is over," exclaimed Richard, joining his two friends on the veranda, "and everything went smoother than I expected."

"Everything went, sure enough," said Mr. Slocum, gloomily; "they all went, - old Giles, and Lumley, and everybody."

"We somewhat expected that, you know."

Thomas Bailey Aldrich

"Yes, I expected it, and wasn't prepared for it."

"It was very bad," said Richard, shaking his head.

The desertion of Giles and his superannuated mates especially touched Mr. Slocum.

"Bad is no word; it was damnable."

"Oh, papa!"

"Pardon me, dear; I couldn't help it. When a man's pensioners throw him over, he must be pretty far gone!"

"The undertow was too strong for them, sir, and they were swept away with the rest. And they all but promised to stay. They will be the very first to come back."

"Of course we shall have to take the old fellows on again," said Mr. Slocum, relenting characteristically.

"Never!" cried Richard.

"I wish I had some of your grit."

"I have none to spare. To tell the truth, when I stood up there to speak, with every eye working on me, like a half-inch drill, I would have sold myself at a low figure."

"But you were a perfect what's-his-name, - Demosthenes," said Mr. Slocum, with a faint smile. "We could hear you."

"I don't believe Demosthenes ever moved an audience as I did mine!" cried Richard gaily. "If his orations produced a like effect, I am certain that the Grecian lecture-bureau never sent him twice to the same place."

"I don't think, Richard, I would engage you over again."

"I am sure Richard spoke very well," interrupted Margaret. "His speech was short" -

"Say shortened, Margaret, for I hadn't got through when they left."

"No, I will not jest about it. It is too serious for jesting. What is to become of the families of all these men suddenly thrown out of employment?"

"They threw themselves out, Mag," said her father.

"That does not mend the matter, papa. There will be great destitution and suffering in the village with every mill closed; and they are all going to close, Bridget says. Thank Heaven that this did not happen in the winter!"

"They always pick their weather," observed Mr. Slocum.

"It will not be for long," said Richard encouragingly. "Our own hands and the spinners, who had no ground for complaint, will return to work shortly, and the managers of the iron mills will have to yield a point or two. In a week at the outside everything will be running smoothly, and on a sounder foundation than before. I believe the strike will be an actual benefit to everybody in the end."

By dint of such arguments and his own sanguine temperament, Richard succeeded in reassuring Mr. Slocum for the time being, though Richard did not hide from himself the gravity of the situation. There was a general strike in the village. Eight hundred men were without work. That meant, or would mean in a few days, two or three thousand women and children without bread. It does not take the wolf long to reach a poor man's door when it is left ajar.

The trades-union had a fund for emergencies of this sort, and some outside aid might be looked for; but such supplies are in their nature precarious and soon exhausted. It is a noticeable feature of strikes that the moment the workman's pay stops his living expenses increase. Even the more economical becomes improvident. If he has money, the tobacco shop and the tavern are likely to get more of it than the butcher's cart. The prolonged strain is too great to be endured without stimulant.

XVII

During the first and second days of the strike, Stillwater presented an animated and even a festive appearance. Throngs of operatives in their Sunday clothes strolled through the streets, or lounged at the corners chatting with other groups; some wandered into the suburbs, and lay in the long grass under the elms. Others again, though these were few, took to the turnpike or the railroad track, and tramped across country.

It is needless to say that the bar-room of the tavern was crowded from early morning down to the hour when the law compelled Mr. Snelling to shut off his gas. After which, John Brown's "soul" could be heard "marching on" in the darkness, through various crooked lanes and alleys, until nearly daybreak.

Among the earliest to scent trouble in the air was Han-Lin, the Chinaman before mentioned. He kept a small laundry in Mud Lane, where his name was painted perpendicularly on a light of glass in the basement window of a tenement house. Han-Lin intended to be buried some day in a sky-blue coffin in his own land, and have a dozen packs of firecrackers decorously exploded over his remains. In order to reserve himself for this and other ceremonies involving the burning of a great quantity of gilt paper, he quietly departed for

Boston at the first sign of popular discontent. As Dexter described it, "Han-Lin coiled up his pig-tail, put forty grains of rice in a yallar bag, - enough to last him a month! - and toddled off in his two-story wooden shoes." He could scarcely have done a wiser thing, for poor Han-Lin's laundry was turned wrong side out within thirty-six hours afterwards.

The strike was popular. The spirit of it spread, as fire and fever and all elemental forces spread. The two apprentices in Brackett's bakery had a dozen minds about striking that first morning. The younger lad, Joe Wiggin, plucked up courage to ask Brackett for a day off, and was lucky enough to dodge a piece of dough weighing nearly four pounds.

Brackett was making bread while the sun shone. He knew that before the week was over there would be no cash customers, and he purposed then to shut up shop.

On the third and fourth days there was no perceptible fall in the barometer. Trade was brisk with Snelling, and a brass band was playing national airs on a staging erected on the green in front of the post-office. Nightly meetings took place at Grimsey's Hall, and the audiences were good-humored and orderly. Torrini advanced some Utopian theories touching a universal distribution of wealth, which were listened to attentively, but failed to produce deep impression.

"That's a healthy idea of Torrini's about dervidin' up property," said Jemmy Willson. "I've heerd it afore; but it's sing'ler I never knowd a feller with any property to have that idea."

" Ther' 's a great dale in it, I can tell ye , " replied

Michael Hennessey, with a well-blackened Woodstock pipe between his teeth and his hands tucked under his coat-tails. "Isn't ther', Misther Stavens?"

When Michael had on his bottle-green swallow-tailed coat with the brass buttons, he invariably assumed a certain lofty air of ceremony in addressing his companions.

"It is sorter pleasant to look at," returned Stevens, "but it don't seem to me an idea that would work. Suppose that, after all the property was divided, a fresh shipload of your friends was to land at New York or Boston; would there be a new deal?"

"No, sir! by no means!" exclaimed Michael excitedly. "The furreners is counted out!"

"But you're a foreigner yourself, Mike."

"Am I, then? Bedad, I'm not! I'm a rale American Know Nothing."

"Well, Mike," said Stevens maliciously, "when it comes to a reg'lar division of lands and greenbacks in the United States, I go in for the Chinese having their share."

"The Chinese!" shouted Michael. "Oh, murther, Misther Stevens! Ye wouldn't be fur dividin' with thim blatherskites!"

"Yes, with them, - as well as the rest," returned Stevens, dryly.

Meanwhile the directors and stockholders of the

various mills took counsel in a room at the rear of the National Bank. Mr. Slocum, following Richard's advice, declined to attend the meeting in person, or to allow his name to figure on the list of vice-presidents.

"Why should we hitch our good cause to their doubtful one?" reflected Richard. "We have no concessions or proposals to make. When our men are ready to come back to us, they will receive just wages and fair treatment. They know that. We do not want to fight the molders. Let the iron-mills do their own fighting;" and Richard stolidly employed himself in taking an account of stock, and forwarding by express to their destination the ten or twelve carved mantel-pieces that happily completed the last contract.

Then his responsibilities shrunk to winding up the office clock and keeping Mr. Slocum firmly on his legs. The latter was by far the more onerous duty, for Mr. Slocum ran down two or three times in the course of every twenty-four hours, while the clock once wound was fixed for the day.

"If I could only have a good set of Waltham works put into your father," said Richard to Margaret, after one of Mr. Slocum's relapses, "he would go better."

"Poor papa! he is not a fighter, like you."

"Your father is what I call a belligerent non-combatant."

Richard was seeing a great deal of Margaret these days. Mr. Slocum had invited him to sleep in the studio until the excitement was past. Margaret was afraid to have him take that long walk between the yard and his lodgings in Lime Street, and then her father was an old man to be without any protection in the house in such untoward times.

So Richard slept in the studio, and had his plate at table, like one of the family. This arrangement was favorable to many a stolen five minutes with Margaret, in the hall or on the staircase. In these fortuitous moments he breathed an atmosphere that sustained him in his task of dispelling Mr. Slocum's recurrent fits of despondency. Margaret had her duties, too, at this period, and the forenoons were sacred to them.

One morning as she passed down the street with a small wicker basket on her arm, Richard said to Mr. Slocum, -

"Margaret has joined the strikers."

The time had already come to Stillwater when many a sharp-faced little urchin - as dear to the warm, deep bosom that had nursed it as though it were a crown prince - would not have had a crust to gnaw if Margaret Slocum had not joined the strikers. Sometimes her heart drooped on the way home from these errands, upon seeing how little of the misery she could ward off. On her rounds there was one cottage in a squalid lane where the children asked for bread in Italian. She never omitted to halt at that door.

"Is it quite prudent for Margaret to be going about so?" queried Mr. Slocum.

"She is perfectly safe," said Richard, - "as safe as a Sister of Charity, which she is."

Indeed, Margaret might then have gone loaded with diamonds through the streets at midnight. There was not a rough man in Stillwater who would not have reached forth an arm to shield her.

"It is costing me nearly as much as it would to carry on the yard," said Mr. Slocum, "but I never put out any stamps more willingly."

"You never took a better contract, sir, than when you agreed to keep Margaret's basket filled. It is an investment in real estate - hereafter."

"I hope so," answered Mr. Slocum, "and I know it's a good thing now."

Of the morals of Stillwater at this time, or at any time, the less said the better. But out of the slime and ooze below sprang the white flower of charity.

The fifth day fell on a Sabbath, and the churches were crowded. The Rev. Arthur Langly selected his text from St. Matthew, chap. xxii, v. 21: "Render therefore unto Cæsar the things which are Cæsar's." But as he did not make it quite plain which was Cæsar, - the trades-union or the Miantowona Iron Works, - the sermon went for nothing, unless it could be regarded as a hint to those persons who had stolen a large piece of belting from the Dana Mills. On the other hand, Father O'Meara that morning bravely told his children to conduct themselves in an orderly manner while they were out of work, or they would catch it in this world and in the next.

On the sixth day a keen observer might have detected a change in the atmosphere. The streets were thronged as usual, and the idlers still wore their Sunday clothes, but the holiday buoyancy of the earlier part of the week had evaporated. A turn-out on the part of one of the trades, though it was accompanied by music and a banner with a lively inscription, failed to arouse general enthusiasm. A serious and even a sullen face was not rare among the crowds that wandered aimlessly up and down the village.

On the seventh day it required no penetration to see the change. There was decidedly less good-natured chaffing and more drunkenness, though Snelling had invoked popular contumely and decimated his bar-room by refusing to trust for drinks. Bracket had let his ovens cool, and his shutters were up. The treasury of the trades-union was nearly drained, and there were growlings that too much had been fooled away on banners and a brass band for the iron men's parade the previous forenoon. It was when Brackett's eye sighted the banner with "Bread or Blood" on it, that he had put up his shutters.

Torrini was now making violent harangues at Grimsey's Hall to largely augmented listeners, whom his words irritated without convincing. Shut off from the tavern, the men flocked to hear him and the other speakers, for born orators were just then as thick as unripe whortleberries. There was nowhere else to go. At home were reproaches that maddened, and darkness, for the kerosene had given out.

Though all the trades had been swept into the movement, it is not to be understood that every workman was losing his head. There were men who owned their cottages and had small sums laid by in the savings-bank; who had always sent their children to

Thomas Bailey Aldrich

the district school, and listened themselves to at least one of Mr. Langly's sermons or one of Father O'Meara's discourses every Sunday. These were anchored to good order; they neither frequented the bar-room nor attended the conclaves at Grimsey's Hall, but deplored as deeply as any one the spirit that was manifesting itself. They would have returned to work now - if they had dared. To this class belonged Stevens.

"Why don't you come up to the hall, nights?" asked Durgin, accosting him on the street, one afternoon. "You'd run a chance of hearing me hold forth some of these evenings."

"You've answered your own question, William. I shouldn't like to see you making an idiot of yourself."

"This is a square fight between labor and capital," returned Durgin with dignity, "and every man ought to take a hand in it."

"William," said Stevens meditatively, "do you know about the Siamese twins?"

"What about 'em, - they're dead, ain't they?" replied Durgin, with surprise.

"I believe so; but when they was alive, if you was to pinch one of those fellows, the other fellow would sing out. If you was to black the eye of the left-hand chap, the right-hand chap wouldn't have been able to see for a week. When either of 'em fetched the other a clip, he knocked himself down. Labor and capital is jined just as those two was. When you've got this fact well into your skull, William, I shall be pleased to listen to your ideas at Grimsey's Hall or anywhere else."

Such conservatism as Stevens's, however, was necessarily swept out of sight for the moment. The wealthier citizens were in a state bordering on panic, - all but Mr. Lemuel Shackford. In his flapping linen duster, for the weather was very sultry now, Mr. Shackford was seen darting excitedly from street to street and hovering about the feverish crowds, like the stormy petrel wheeling on the edges of a gale. Usually as chary of his sympathies as of his gold, he astonished every one by evincing an abnormal interest in the strikers. The old man declined to put down anything on the subscription paper then circulating; but he put down his sympathies to any amount. He held no stock in the concerns involved; he hated Slocum, and he hated the directors of the Miantowona Iron Works. The least he hoped was that Rowland Slocum would be laid out.

So far the strikers had committed no overt act of note, unless it was the demolition of Han-Lin's laundry. Stubbs, the provision dealer, had been taught the rashness of exposing samples of potatoes in his doorway, and the "Tonsorial Emporium" of Professor Brown, a colored citizen, had been invaded by two humorists, who, after having their hair curled, refused to pay for it, and the professor had been too agitated to insist. The story transpiring, ten or twelve of the boys had dropped in during the morning, and got shaved on the same terms. "By golly, gen'l'men!" expostulated the professor, "ef dis yah thing goes on, dis darkey will be cleaned cl'ar out fo de week's done." No act of real violence had been perpetrated as yet; but with bands of lawless men roaming over the village at all hours of the day and night, the situation was critical.

The wheel of what small social life there was in Stillwater had ceased to revolve. With the single exception of Lemuel Shackford, the more respectable inhabitants kept in-doors as much as practicable. From the first neither Mr. Craggie nor Lawyer Perkins had gone to the hotel to consult the papers in the reading-room, and Mr. Pinkham did not dare to play on his flute of an evening. The Rev. Arthur Langly found it politic to do but little visiting in the parish. His was not the pinion to buffet with a wind like this, and indeed he was not explicitly called upon to do so. He sat sorrowfully in his study day by day, preparing the weekly sermon, - a gentle, pensive person, inclined in the best of weather to melancholia. If Mr. Langly had gone into arboriculture instead of into the ministry, he would have planted nothing but weeping-willows.

In the mean time the mill directors continued their deliberations in the bank building, and had made several abortive attempts to effect an arrangement with the leaders of the union. This seemed every hour less possible and more necessary.

On the afternoon of the seventh day of the strike a crowd gathered in front of the residence of Mr. Alexander, the superintendent of the Miantowona Iron Works, and began groaning and hooting. Mr. Alexander sought out Mr. Craggie, and urged him, as a man of local weight and one accustomed to addressing the populace, to speak a few words to the mob. That was setting Mr. Craggie on the horns of a cruel dilemma. He was afraid to disoblige the representative of so powerful a corporation as the Miantowona Iron Works, but he equally dreaded to risk his popularity with seven or eight hundred voters; so, like the crafty chancellor in Tennyson's poem, he dallied with his golden chain, and, smiling, but the question by.

"Drat the man!" muttered Mr. Craggie, "does he want to blast my whole political career! *I* can't pitch into our adopted countrymen."

There was a blot on the escutcheon of Mr. Craggie which he was very anxious not to have uncovered by any chance in these latter days, - his ancient affiliation with the deceased native American party.

The mob dispersed without doing damage, but the fact that it had collected and had shown an ugly temper sent a thrill of apprehension through the village. Mr. Slocum came in a great flurry to Richard.

"This thing ought to be stopped," said Mr. Slocum.

"I agree to that," replied Richard, bracing himself not to agree to anything else.

"If we were to drop that stipulation as to the increase of apprentices, no doubt many of the men would give over insisting on an advance."

"Our only salvation is to stick to our right to train as many workmen as we choose. The question of wages is of no account compared with that; the rate of wages will adjust itself."

"If we could manage it somehow with the marble workers," suggested Mr. Slocum, "that would demoralize the other trades, and they'd be obliged to fall in."

"I don't see that they lack demoralization."

"If something isn't done, they'll end up by knocking in our front doors or burning us all up."

"Let them."

"It's very well to say let them," exclaimed Mr. Slocum, petulantly, "when you haven't any front door to be knocked in!"

"But I have you and Margaret to consider, if there were actual danger. When anything like violence threatens, there's an honest shoulder for every one of the hundred and fifty muskets in the armory."

"Those muskets might get on the wrong shoulders."

"That isn't likely. You do not seem to know, sir, that there is a strong guard at the armory day and night."

"I was not aware of that."

"It is a fact all the same," said Richard; and Mr. Slocum went away easier in his mind, and remained so - two or three hours.

On the eighth, ninth, and tenth days the clouds lay very black along the horizon. The marble workers, who began to see their mistake, were reproaching the foundry men with enticing them into to coalition, and the spinners were hot in their denunciations of the molders. Ancient personal antagonisms that had been slumbering started to their feet. Torrini fell out of favor, and in the midst of one of his finest perorations uncomplimentary missiles, selected from the animal kingdom, had been thrown at him. The grand torchlight procession on the night of the ninth culminated in a disturbance, in which many men got injured, several badly, and the windows of Brackett's bakery were stove in. A point of light had pierced the darkness, - the trades were quarreling among themselves!

The selectmen had sworn in special constables among the citizens, and some of the more retired streets were now patrolled after dark, for there had been threats of incendiarism.

Bishop's stables burst into flames one midnight, - whether fired intentionally or accidentally was not known; but the giant bellows at Dana's Mills was slit and two belts were cut at the Miantowona Iron Works that same night.

At this juncture a report that out-of-town hands were coming to replace the strikers acted on the public mind like petroleum on fire. A large body of workmen assembled near the railway station, - to welcome them. There was another rumor which caused the marble workers to stare at each other aghast. It was to the effect that Mr. Slocum, having long meditated retiring from business, had now decided to do so, and was consulting with Wyndham, the keeper of the green-house, about removing the division wall and turning the marble yard into a peach garden. This was an unlooked-for solution of the difficulty. Stillwater without any Slocum's Marble Yard was chaos come again.

"Good Lord, boys!" cried Piggott, "if Slocum should do that!"

Meanwhile, Snelling's bar had been suppressed by the

Thomas Bailey Aldrich

authorities, and a posse of policemen, borrowed from South Millville, occupied the premises. Knots of beetle-browed men, no longer in holiday gear, but chiefly in their shirt-sleeves, collected from time to time at the head of the main street, and glowered threateningly at the single policeman pacing the porch of the tavern. The Stillwater Grays were under arms in the armory over Dundon's drugstore. The thoroughfare had ceased to be safe for any one, and Margaret's merciful errands were necessarily brought to an end. How the poor creatures who had depended on her bounty now continued to exist was a sorrowful problem.

Matters were at this point, when on the morning of the thirteenth day Richard noticed the cadaverous face of a man peering into the yard through the slats of the main gate. Richard sauntered down there, with his hands in his pockets. The man was old Giles, and with him stood Lumley and Peterson, gazing thoughtfully at the sign outside, -

NO ADMITTANCE EXCEPT ON BUSINESS.

The roughly lettered clapboard, which they had heedlessly passed a thousand times, seemed to have taken a novel significance to them.

Richard. What's wanted there?

Giles. [Very affably.] We was lookin' round for a job, Mr. Shackford.

Richard. We are not taking on any hands at present.

Giles. Didn't know but you was. Somebody said

you was.

Richard. Somebody is mistaken.

Giles. P'rhaps to-morrow, or nex' day?

Richard. Rather doubtful, Giles.

Giles. [Uneasily.] Mr. Slocum ain't goin' to give up business, is he?

Richard. Why shouldn't he, if it doesn't pay? The business is carried on for his amusement and profit; when the profit stops it won't be amusing any longer. Mr. Slocum is not going to run the yard for the sake of the Marble Workers' Association. He would rather drive a junk-cart. He might be allowed to steer that himself.

Giles. Oh!

Richard. Good-morning, Giles.

Gikles. 'Mornin', Mr. Shackford.

Richard rushed back to Mr. Slocum.

"The strike is broken, sir!"

"What do you mean?"

"The thing has collapsed! The tide is turning, *and has washed in a lot of dead wood!"*

"Thank God!" cried Mr. Slocum.

An hour or so later a deputation of four, consisting of Stevens, Denyven, Durgin, and Piggott, waited upon Mr. Slocum in his private office, and offered, on behalf of all the departments, to resume work at the old rates.

Mr. Slocum replied that he had not objected to the old rates, but the new, and that he accepted their offer - conditionally.

"You have overlooked one point, Mr. Stevens."

"Which one, sir?"

"The apprentices."

"We thought you might not insist there, sir."

"I insist on conducting my own business in my own way."

The voice was the voice of Slocum, but the backbone was Richard's.

"Then, sir, the Association don't object to a reasonable number of apprentices."

"How many is that?"

"As many as you want, I expect, sir," said Stevens, shuffling his feet.

"Very well, Stevens. Go round to the front gate and Mr. Shackford will let you in."

There were two doors to the office, one leading into the yard, and the other, by which the deputation had entered and was now making its exit, opened upon the street.

Richard heaved a vast sigh of relief as he took down the beam securing the principal entrance.

"Good-morning, boys," he chirped, with a smile as bright as newly minted gold. "I hope you enjoyed yourselves."

The quartet ducked their heads bashfully, and Stevens replied, "Can't speak for the others, Mr. Shackford, but I never enjoyed myself worse."

Piggott lingered a moment behind the rest, and looking back over his shoulder said, "That peach garden was what fetched us!"

Richard gave a loud laugh, for the peach garden had been a horticultural invention of his own.

In the course of the forenoon the majority of the hands presented themselves at the office, dropping into the yard in gangs of five or six, and nearly all were taken on. To dispose definitely of Lumley, Giles, and Peterson, they were not taken on at Slocum's Yard, though they continued to be, directly or indirectly, Slocum's pensioners, even after they were retired to the town farm.

Once more the chisels sounded merrily under the long shed. That same morning the spinners went back to the mules, but the molders held out until nightfall, when it was signified to them that they demands would be complied with.

The next day the steam-whistles of the Miantowona Iron Works and Dana's Mills sent the echoes flying beyond that undulating line of pines and hemlocks which half encircles Stillwater, and falls away loosely on either side, like an unclasped girdle.

A calm, as if from out the cloudless blue sky that arched it day after day, seemed to drift down upon the village. Han-Lin, with no more facial expression than an orange, suddenly reappeared on the streets, and went about repairing his laundry, unmolested. The children were playing in the sunny lanes again, unafraid, and mothers sat on doorsteps in the summer twilights, singing softly to the baby in arm. There was meat on the table, and the tea-kettle hummed comfortably at the back of the stove. The very winds that rustled through the fragrant pines, and wandered fitfully across the vivid green of the salt marshes, breathed peace and repose.

Then, one morning, this blissful tranquility was rudely shattered. Old Mr. Lemuel Shackford had been found murdered in his own house in Welch's Court.

XVIII

The general effect on Stillwater of Mr. Shackford's death and the peculiar circumstances attending the tragedy have been set forth in the earlier chapters of this narrative. The influence which that event exerted upon several persons then but imperfectly known to the reader is now to occupy us.

On the conclusion of the strike, Richard had returned, in the highest spirits, to his own rooms in Lime Street; but the quiet week that followed found him singularly depressed. His nerves had been strung to their utmost tension during those thirteen days of suspense; he had assumed no light responsibility in the matter of closing the yard, and there had been moments when the task of sustaining Mr. Slocum had appeared almost hopeless. Now that the strain was removed a reaction set in, and Richard felt himself unnerved by the fleeing shadow of the trouble which had not caused him to flinch so long as it faced him.

On the morning and at the moment when Mary Hennessey was pushing open the scullery door of the house in Welch's Court, and was about to come upon the body of the forlorn old man lying there in his night-dress, Richard sat eating his breakfast in a silent and preoccupied mood. He had retired very late the previous night, and his lack-lustre eyes showed the effect of insufficient sleep. His single fellow-boarder, Mr. Pinkham, had not returned from his customary early walk, and only Richard and Mrs. Spooner, the landlady, were at table. The former was in the act of lifting the coffee-cup to his lips, when the schoolmaster burst excitedly into the room.

"Old Mr. Shackford is dead!" he exclaimed, dropping into a chair near the door. "There's a report down in the village that he has been murdered. I don't know if it is true. . . . . God forgive my abruptness! I didn't think!" and Mr. Pinkham turned an apologetic face towards Richard, who sat there deathly pale, holding the cup rigidly within an inch or two of his lip, and staring blankly into space like a statue.

"I - I ought to have reflected," murmured the schoolmaster, covered with confusion at his maladroitness. "It was very reprehensible in Craggie to make such an announcement to me so suddenly, on a street corner. I - I was quite upset by it."

Richard pushed back his chair without replying, and passed into the hall, where he encountered a messenger from Mr. Slocum, confirming Mr. Pinkham's intelligence, but supplementing it with the rumor that Lemuel Shackford had committed suicide.

Richard caught up his hat from a table, and hurried to Welch's Court. Before reaching the house he had somewhat recovered his outward composure; but he was still pale and internally much agitated, for he had received a great shock, as Lawyer Perkins afterwards observed to Mr. Ward in the reading-room of the tavern. Both these gentlemen were present when Richard arrived, as were also several of the immediate neighbors and two constables. The latter were guarding the door against the crowd, which had already begun to collect in the front yard.

A knot of carpenters, with their tool-boxes on their shoulders, had halted at the garden gate on their way to Bishop's new stables, and were glancing curiously at the unpainted façade of the house, which seemed to have taken on a remote, bewildered expression, as if it had an inarticulate sense of the horror within. The men ceased their whispered conversation as Richard approached, and respectfully moved aside to let him pass.

Nothing had been changed in the cheerless room on the ground floor, with its veneered mahogany furniture and its yellowish leprous wall-paper, peeling off at the seams here and there. A cane-seated chair, overturned near the table, had been left untouched, and the body was still lying in the position in which the Hennessey girl had discovered it. A strange chill - something unlike any atmospherical sharpness, a chill that seemed to exhale from the thin, pinched nostrils - permeated the apartment. The orioles were singing madly outside, their vermilion bosoms glowing like live coals against the tender green of the foliage, and appearing to break into flame as they took sudden flights hither and thither; but within all was still. On entering the chamber Richard was smitten by the silence, - that silence which shrouds the dead, and is like no other. Lemuel Shackford had not been kind or cousinly; he had blighted Richard's childhood with harshness and neglect, and had lately heaped cruel insult upon him; but as he stood there alone, and gazed for a moment at the firmly shut lips, upon which the mysterious white dust of death had already settled, - the lips that were never to utter any more bitter things, - the tears gathered in Richard's eyes and ran slowly down his cheeks. After all said and done, Lemuel Shackford was his kinsman, and blood is thicker than water!

Coroner Whidden shortly appeared on the scene, accompanied by a number of persons; a jury was impaneled, and then began that inquest which resulted in shedding so very little light on the catastrophe.

The investigation completed, there were endless details to attend to, - papers to be hurriedly examined and sealed, and arrangements made for the funeral on the succeeding day. These matters occupied Richard until late in the afternoon, when he retired to his lodgings, looking in on Margaret for a few minutes on his way home.

"This is too dreadful!" said Margaret, clinging to his hand, with fingers nearly as icy as his own.

"It is unspeakably sad," answered Richard, - "the saddest thing I ever knew."

"Who - who could have been so cruel?"

Richard shook his head.

"No one knows."

The funeral took place on Thursday, and on Friday morning, as has been stated, Mr. Taggett arrived in Stillwater, and installed himself in Welch's Court, to the wonder of many in the village, who would not have slept a night in that house, with only a servant in the north gable, for half the universe. Mr. Taggett was a person who did not allow himself to be swayed by his imagination.

Here, then, he began his probing of a case which, on the surface, promised to be a very simple one. The man who had been seen driving rapidly along the turnpike sometime near daybreak, on Wednesday, was presumably the man who could tell him all about it. But it did not prove so. Neither Thomas Blufton, nor William Durgin, nor any of the tramps subsequently obliged to drop into autobiography could be connected with the affair.

These first failures served to stimulate Mr. Taggett; it required a complex case to stir his ingenuity and sagacity. That the present was not a complex case he was still convinced, after four days' futile labor upon it. Mr. Shackford had been killed - either with malice prepense or on the spur of the moment - for his money. The killing had likely enough not been premeditated; the old man had probably opposed the robbery. Now, among the exceptionally rough population of the town there were possibly fifty men who would not have hesitated to strike down Mr. Shackford if he had caught them *flagrante delicto* and resisted them, or attempted to call for succor. That the crime was committed by some one in Stillwater or in the neighborhood Mr. Taggett had never doubted since the day of his arrival. The clumsy manner in which the staple had been wrenched from the scullery door showed the absence of a professional hand. Then the fact that the deceased was in the habit of keeping money in his bedchamber was a fact well known in the village, and not likely to be known outside of it, though of course it might have been. It was clearly necessary for Mr. Taggett to carry his investigation into the workshops

Thomas Bailey Aldrich

and among the haunts of the class which was indubitably to furnish him with the individual he wanted. Above all, it was necessary that the investigation should be secret. An obstacle obtruded itself here: everybody in Stillwater knew everybody, and a stranger appearing on the streets or dropping frequently into the tavern would not escape comment.

The man with the greatest facility for making the requisite searches would of course be some workman. But a workman was the very agent not to be employed under the circumstances. How many times, and by what strange fatality, had a guilty party been selected to shadow his own movements, or those of an accomplice! No, Mr. Taggett must rely only on himself, and his plan forthwith matured. Its execution, however, was delayed several days, the cooperation of Mr. Slocum and Mr. Richard Shackford being indispensable.

At this stage Richard went to New York, where his cousin had made extensive investments in real estate. For a careful man, the late Mr. Shackford had allowed his affairs there to become strangely tangled. The business would detain Richard a fortnight.

Three days after his departure Mr. Taggett himself left Stillwater, having apparently given up the case; a proceeding which was severely criticized, not only in the columns of The Stillwater Gazette, but by the townsfolks at large, who immediately relapsed into a state of apprehension approximating that of the morning when the crime was discovered. Mr. Pinkham, who was taking tea that evening at the Danas', threw the family into a panic by asserting his belief that this was merely the first of a series of artistic assassinations in the manner of those Memorable Murders recorded by De Quincey. Mr. Pinkham may have said this to impress the four Dana girls with the variety of his reading, but the recollection of De Quincey's harrowing paper had the effect of so unhinging the young school-master that when he found himself, an hour or two afterwards, in the lonely, unlighted street he flitted home like a belated ghost, and was ready to drop at every tree-box.

The next forenoon a new hand was taken on at Slocum's Yard. The new hand, who had come on foot from South Millville, at which town he had been set down by the seven o'clock express that morning, was placed in the apprentice department, - there were five or six apprentices now. Though all this was part of an understood arrangement, Mr. Slocum nearly doubted the fidelity of his own eyes when Mr. Taggett, a smooth-faced young fellow of one and twenty, if so old, with all the traits of an ordinary workman down to the neglected fingernails, stepped up to the desk to have the name of Blake entered on the pay-roll. Either by chance or by design, Mr. Taggett had appeared but seldom on the streets of Stillwater; the few persons who had had anything like familiar intercourse with him in his professional capacity were precisely the persons with whom his present movements were not likely to bring him into juxtaposition, and he ran slight risk of recognition by others. With his hair closely cropped, and the overhanging brown mustache removed, the man was not so much disguised as transformed. "I shouldn't have known him!" muttered Mr. Slocum, as he watched Mr. Taggett passing from the office with his hat in his hand. During the ensuing ten or twelve days Mr. Slocum never wholly succeeded in extricating himself from the foggy uncertainty generated by that one brief interview. From the moment Mr. Taggett was assigned a bench under the sheds, Mr. Slocum saw little or nothing of him.

Mr. Taggett took lodging in a room in one of the most crowded of the low boarding-houses, - a room accommodating two beds besides his own: the first occupied by a brother neophyte in marble-cutting, and the second by a morose middle-aged man with one eyebrow a trifle higher than the other, as if it had been wrenched out of line by the strain of habitual intoxication. This man's name was Wollaston, and he worked at Dana's.

Mr. Taggett's initial move was to make himself popular in the marble yard, and especially at the tavern, where he spent money freely, though not so freely as to excite any remark except that the lad was running through pretty much all his small pay, - a recklessness which was charitably condoned in Snelling's bar-room. He formed multifarious friendships, and had so many sensible views on the labor problem, advocating the general extinguishment of capitalists, and so on, that his admittance to the Marble Workers' Association resolved itself into merely a question of time. The old prejudice against apprentices was already wearing off. The quiet, evasive man of few words was now a loquacious talker, holding his own with the hardest hitters, and very skillful in giving offense to no one. "Whoever picks up Blake for a fool," Dexter remarked one night, "will put him down again." Not a shadow of suspicion followed Mr. Taggett in his various comings and goings. He seemed merely a good-natured, intelligent devil; perhaps a little less devilish and a trifle more intelligent than the rest, but not otherwise different. Denyven, Peters,

Dexter, Willson, and others in and out of the Slocum clique were Blake's sworn friends. In brief, Mr. Taggett had the amplest opportunities to prosecute his studies. Only for a pained look which sometimes latterly shot into his eyes, as he worked at the bench, or as he walked alone in the street, one would have imagined that he was thoroughly enjoying the half-vagabond existence.

The supposition would have been erroneous, for in the progress of those fourteen days' apprenticeship Mr. Taggett had received a wound in the most sensitive part of his nature: he had been forced to give up what no man ever relinquishes without a wrench, - his own idea.

With the exception of an accident in Dana's Mill, by which Torrini's hand had been so badly mangled that amputation was deemed necessary, the two weeks had been eventless outside of Mr. Taggett's personal experience. What that experience was will transpire in its proper place. Margaret was getting daily notes from Richard, and Mr. Slocum, overburdened with the secret of Mr. Taggett's presence in the yard, - a secret confined exclusively to Mr. Slocum, Richard, and Justice Beemis, - was restlessly awaiting developments.

The developments came that afternoon when Mr. Taggett walked into the office and startled Mr. Slocum, sitting at the desk. The two words which Mr. Taggett then gravely and coldly whispered in Mr. Slocum's ear were, -

"RICHARD SHACKFORD."

XIX

Mr. Slocum, who had partly risen from the chair, sank back into his seat. "Good God!" he said, turning very pale. "Are you mad?"

Mr. Taggett realized the cruel shock which the pronouncing of that name must have caused Mr. Slocum. Mr. Taggett had meditated his line of action, and had decided that the most merciful course was brusquely to charge young Shackford with the crime, and allow Mr. Slocum to sustain himself for a while with the indignant disbelief which would be natural to him, situated as he was. He would then in a manner be prepared for the revelations which, if suddenly presented, would crush him.

If Mr. Taggett was without imagination, as he claimed, he was not without a certain feminine quickness of sympathy often found in persons engaged in professions calculated to blunt the finer sensibilities. In his intercourse with Mr. Slocum at the Shackford house, Mr. Taggett had been won by the singular gentleness and simplicity of the man, and was touched by his misfortune.

After his exclamation, Mr. Slocum did not speak for a moment or two, but with his elbows resting on the edge of the desk sat motionless, like a person stunned.

Then he slowly lifted his face, to which the color had returned, and making a movement with his right hand as if he were sweeping away cobwebs in front of him rose from the chair.

"You are simply mad," he said, looking Mr. Taggett squarely and calmly in the eyes. "Are you aware of Mr. Richard Shackford's character and his position here?"

"Precisely."

"Do you know that he is to marry my daughter?"

"I am very sorry for you, sir."

"You may spare me that. It is quite unnecessary. You have fallen into some horrible delusion. I hope you will be able to explain it."

"I am prepared to do so, sir."

"Are you serious?"

"Very serious, Mr. Slocum."

"You actually imagine that Richard Shackford - Pshaw! It's simply impossible!"

"I am too young a man to wish even to seem wiser than you, but my experience has taught me that nothing is impossible."

"I begin to believe so myself. I suppose you have grounds, or something you consider grounds, for your monstrous suspicion. What are they? I demand to be fully informed of what you have been doing in the yard, before you bring disgrace upon me and my family by inconsiderately acting on some wild theory which perhaps ten words can refute."

"I should be in the highest degree criminal, Mr. Slocum, if I were to make so fearful an accusation against any man unless I had the most incontestable evidence in my hands."

Mr. Taggett spoke with such cold-blooded conviction that a chill crept over Mr. Slocum, in spite of him.

"What is the nature of this evidence?"

"Up to the present stage, purely circumstantial."

"I can imagine that," said Mr. Slocum, with a slight smile.

"But so conclusive as to require no collateral evidence. The testimony of an eye-witness of the crime could scarcely add to my knowledge of what occurred that Tuesday night in Lemuel Shackford's house."

"Indeed, it is all so clear! But of course a few eye-witnesses will turn up eventually," said Mr. Slocum, whose whiteness about the lips discounted the assurance of his sarcasm.

"That is not improbable," returned Mr. Taggett.

"And meanwhile what are the facts?"

"They are not easily stated. I have kept a record of my work day by day, since the morning I entered the yard. The memoranda are necessarily confused, the important and the unimportant being jumbled together; but the record as it stands will answer your question more fully than I could, even if I had the time - which I have not - to go over the case with you. I can leave these notes in your hands, if you desire it. When I return from New York" -

"You are going to New York!" exclaimed Mr. Slocum, with a start. "When?"

"This evening."

"If you lay a finger on Richard Shackford, you will make the mistake of your life, Mr. Taggett!"

"I have other business there. Mr. Shackford will be in Stillwater to-morrow night. He engaged a state-room on the Fall River boat this morning."

"How can you know that?"

"Since last Tuesday none of his movements have been unknown to me."

"Do you mean to say that you have set your miserable spies upon him?" cried Mr. Slocum.

"I should not state the fact in just those words," Mr. Taggett answered. "The fact remains."

"Pardon me," said Mr. Slocum. "I am not quite myself. Can you wonder at it?"

"I do not wonder."

"Give me those papers you speak of, Mr. Taggett. I

Thomas Bailey Aldrich

would like to look through them. I see that you are a very obstinate person when you have once got a notion into your head. Perhaps I can help you out of your error before it is irreparable." Then, after hesitating a second, Mr. Slocum added, "I may speak of this to my daughter? Indeed, I could scarcely keep it from her."

"Perhaps it is better she should be informed."

"And Mr. Shackford, when he returns to-morrow?"

"If he broaches the subject of his cousin's death, I advise you to avoid it."

"Why should I?"

"It might save you or Miss Slocum some awkward-ness, - but you must use your own discretion. As the matter stands it makes no difference whether Mr. Shackford knows his position to-day or to-morrow. It is too late for him to avail himself of the knowledge. Otherwise, of course, I should not have given myself away in this fashion."

"Very well," said Mr. Slocum, with an impatient movement of his shoulders; "neither I nor my daughter will open our lips on this topic. In the mean while you are to take no further steps without advising me. That is understood?"

"That is perfectly understood," returned Mr. Taggett, drawing a narrow red note-book from the inner pocket of his workman's blouse, and producing at the same time a small nickel-plated door-key. "This is the key of Mr. Shackford's private workshop in the extension. I have not been able to replace it on the mantel-shelf of his sitting-room in Lime Street. Will you have the kindness to see that it is done at once?"

A moment later Mr. Slocum stood alone in the office, with Mr. Taggett's diary in his hand. It was one of those costly little volumes - gilt-edged and bound in fragrant crushed Levant morocco - with which city officials are annually supplied by a community of grateful taxpayers.

The dark crimson of the flexible covers, as soft and slippery to the touch as a snake's skin, was perhaps the fitting symbol of the darker story that lay coiled within. With a gesture of repulsion, as if some such fancy had flitted through his mind, Mr. Slocum tossed the note-book on the desk in front of him, and stood a few minutes moodily watching the *reflets* of the crinkled leather as the afternoon sunshine struck across it. Beneath his amazement and indignation he had been chilled to the bone by Mr. Taggett's brutal confidence. It was enough to chill one, surely; and in spite of himself Mr. Slocum began to feel a certain indefinable dread of that little crimson-bound book.

Whatever it contained, the reading of those pages was to be a repellent task to him; it was a task to which he could not bring himself at the moment; to-night, in the privacy of his own chamber, he would sift Mr. Taggett's baleful fancies. Thus temporizing, Mr. Slocum dropped the volume into his pocket, locked the office door behind him, and wandered down to Dundon's drug-store to kill the intervening hour before supper-time. Dundon's was the aristocratic lounging place of the village, - the place where the only genuine Havana cigars in Stillwater were to be had, and where the favored few , the initiated , could get a dash of hochheimer or cognac with their soda-water.

At supper, that evening, Mr. Slocum addressed scarcely a word to Margaret, and Margaret was also silent. The days were dragging heavily with her; she was missing Richard. Her own daring travels had never extended beyond Boston or Providence; and New York, with Richard in it, seemed drearily far away. Mr. Slocum withdrew to his chamber shortly after nine o'clock, and, lighting the pair of candles on the dressing-table, began his examination of Mr. Taggett's memoranda.

At midnight the watchman on his lonely beat saw those two candles still burning.

XX

Mr. Taggett's diary was precisely a diary, - disjoined, full of curt, obscure phrases and irrelevant reflections, - for which reason it will not be reproduced here. Though Mr. Slocum pondered every syllable, and now and then turned back painfully to reconsider some doubtful passage, it is not presumed that the reader will care to do so. An abstract of the journal, with occasional quotation where the writer's words seem to demand it, will be sufficient for the narrative.

In the opening pages Mr. Taggett described his novel surroundings with a minuteness which contrasted oddly with the brief, hurried entries further on. He found himself, as he had anticipated, in a society composed of some of the most heterogeneous elements. Stillwater, viewed from a certain point, was a sort of microcosm, a little international rag-fair to which nearly every country on earth had contributed one of its shabby human products. "I am moving," wrote Mr. Taggett, "in an atmosphere in which any crime is possible. I give myself seven days at the outside to light upon the traces of Shackford's murder. I feel him in the air." The writer's theory was that the man would betray his identity in one of two ways: either by talking unguardedly, or by indulging in expenditures not warranted by his means and position. If several persons had been concerned in the crime, nothing was more likely than a disagreement over the spoil, and consequent treachery on the part of one of them. Or, again, some of the confederates might become alarmed, and attempt to save themselves by giving away their comrades. Mr. Taggett, however, leaned to the belief that the assassin had had no accomplices.

The sum taken from Mr. Shackford's safe was a comparatively large one, - five hundred dollars in gold and nearly double that amount in bank-notes. Neither the gold nor the paper bore any known mark by which it could be recognized; the burglar had doubtless assured himself of this, and would not hesitate to disburse the money. That was even a safer course, judiciously worked, than to secrete it. The point was, Would he have sufficient self-control to get rid of it by degrees? The chances, Mr. Taggett argued, were ten to one he would not.

A few pages further on Mr. Taggett compliments the Unknown on the adroit manner in which he is conducting himself. He has neither let slip a suspicious word, nor made an incautious display of his booty. Snelling's bar was doing an unusually light business. No one appeared to have any money. Many of the men had run deeply into debt during the late strike, and were now drinking moderately. In the paragraph which closes the week's record Mr. Taggett's chagrin is evident. He confesses that he is at fault. "My invisible friend does not *materialize* so successfully as I expected," is Mr. Taggett's comment.

His faith in the correctness of his theory had not abated; but he continued his observation sin a less sanguine spirit. These observations were not limited to the bar-room or the workshop; he informed himself of the domestic surroundings of his comrades. Where his own scrutiny could not penetrate, he employed the aid of correspondents. He knew what workmen had money in the local savings-bank, and the amount of each deposit. In the course of his explorations of the shady side of Stillwater life, Mr. Taggett unearthed many amusing and many pathetic histories, but nothing that served his end. Finally, he began to be discouraged.

Returning home from the tavern, one night, in a rather desponding mood, he found the man Wollaston smoking his pipe in bed. Wollaston was a taciturn man generally, but this night he was conversational, and Mr. Taggett, too restless to sleep, fell to chatting with him. Did he know much about the late Mr. Shackford? Yes, he had known him well enough, in an off way, - not to speak of him; everybody knew him in Stillwater; he was a sort of miser, hated everybody, and bullied everybody. It was a wonder somebody didn't knock the old silvertop on the head years ago.

Thus Mr. Wollaston grimly, with his pores stopped up with iron-fillings, - a person to whom it would come quite easy to knock any one on the head for a slight difference of opinion. He amused Mr. Taggett in his present humor.

No, he wasn't aware that Shackford had had trouble with any particular individual; believed he did have a difficulty once with Slocum, the marble man; but he was always fetching suits against the town and shying lawyers at the mill directors, - a disagreeable old cuss altogether. Adopted his cousin, one time, but made the house so hot for him that the lad ran off to sea, and since then had had nothing to do with the old bilk.

Indeed! What sort of fellow was young Shackford? Mr. Wollaston could not say of his own knowledge; thought him a plucky chap; he had put a big Italian named Torrini out of the yard, one day, for talking back. Who was Torrini? The man that got hurt last week in the Dana Mill. Who were Richard Shackford's intimates? Couldn't say; had seen him with Mr. Pinkham, the school-master, and Mr. Craggie, - went with the upper crust generally. Was going to be partner in the marble yard and marry Slocum's daughter. Will Durgin knew him. They lived together one time. He, Wollaston, was going to turn in now.

Several of these facts were not new to Mr. Taggett, but Mr. Wollaston's presentation of them threw Mr. Taggett into a reverie.

The next evening he got Durgin alone in a corner of the bar-room. With two or three potations Durgin became autobiographical. Was he acquainted with Mr. Shackford outside the yard? Rather. Dick Shackford? His (Durgin's) mother had kept Dick from starving when he was a baby, - and no thanks for it. Went to school with him, and knew all about his running off to sea. Was near going with him. Old man Shackford never liked Dick, who was a proud beggar; they couldn't pull together, down to the last, - both of a piece. They had a jolly rumpus a little while before the old man was fixed.

Mr. Taggett pricked up his ears at this.

A rumpus? How did Durgin know that? A girl told him. What girl? A girl he was sweet on. What was her name? Well, he didn't mind telling her name; it was Molly Hennessey. She was going through Welch's

Court one forenoon, - may be it was three days before the strike, - and saw Dick Shackford bolt out of the house, swinging his arms and swearing to himself at an awful rate. Was Durgin certain that Molly Hennessey had told him this? Yes, he was ready to take his oath on it.

Here, at last, was something that looked like a glimmer of daylight.

It was possible that Durgin or the girl had lied; but the story had an air of truth to it. If it were a fact that there had recently been a quarrel between these cousins, whose uncousinly attitude towards each other was fast becoming clear to Mr. Taggett, then here was a conceivable key to an enigma which had puzzled him.

The conjecture that Lemuel Shackford had himself torn up the will - if it was a will, for this still remained in dispute - had never been satisfactory to Mr. Taggett. He had accepted it because he was unable to imagine an ordinary burglar pausing in the midst of his work to destroy a paper in which he could have no concern. But Richard Shackford would have the liveliest possible interest in the destruction of a document that placed a vast estate beyond his reach. Here was a motive on a level with the crime. That money had been taken, and that the fragments of the will had been carelessly thrown into a waste-paper basket, just as if the old man himself had thrown them there, was a stroke of art which Mr. Taggett admired more and more as he reflected upon it.

He did not, however, allow himself to lay too much stress on these points; for the paper might turn out to be merely an expired lease, and the girl might have

Thomas Bailey Aldrich

been quizzing Durgin. Mr. Taggett would have given one of his eye-teeth just then for ten minutes with Mary Hennessey. But an interview with her at this stage was neither prudent nor easily compassed.

"If I have not struck a trail," writes Mr. Taggett, "I have come upon what strongly resembles one; the least I can do is to follow it. My first move must be to inspect that private workshop in the rear of Mr. Slocum's house. How shall I accomplish it? I cannot apply to him for permission, for that would provoke questions which I am not ready to answer. Moreover, I have yet to assure myself that Mr. Slocum is not implicated. There seems to have been also a hostile feeling existing between him and the deceased. Why didn't some one tell me these things at the start! If young Shackford is the person, there is a tangled story to be unraveled. *Mem:* Young Shackford is Miss Slocum's lover."

Mr. Slocum read this passage twice without drawing breath, and then laid down the book an instant to wipe the sudden perspiration from his forehead.

In the note which followed, Mr. Taggett described the difficulty he met with in procuring a key to fit the wall-door at the rear of the marble yard, and gave an account of his failure to effect an entrance into the studio. He had hoped to find a window unfastened; but the window, as well as the door opening upon the veranda, was locked, and in the midst of his operations, which were conducted at noon-time, the approach of a servant had obliged him to retreat.

Forced to lay aside, at least temporarily, his designs on the workshop, he turned his attention to Richard's lodgings in Lime Street. Here Mr. Taggett was more successful. On the pretext that he had been sent for certain drawings which were to be found on the table or in a writing-desk, he was permitted by Mrs. Spooner to ascend to the bedroom, where she obligingly insisted on helping him search for the apocryphal plans, and seriously interfered with his purpose, which was to find the key of the studio. While Mr. Taggett was turning over the pages of a large dictionary, in order to gain time, and was wondering how he could rid himself of the old lady's importunities, he came upon a half-folded note-sheet, at the bottom of which his eye caught the name of Lemuel Shackford. It was in the handwriting of the dead man. Mr. Taggett was very familiar with that handwriting. He secured the paper at a venture, and put it in his pocket without examination.

A few minutes later, it being impossible to prolong the pretended quest for the drawings, Mr. Taggett was obliged to follow Mrs. Spooner from the apartment. As he did so he noticed a bright object lying on the corner of the mantel-shelf, - a small nickel-plated key. In order to take it he had only to reach out his hand in passing. It was, as Mr. Taggett had instantly surmised, the key of Richard's workshop.

If it had been gold, instead of brass or iron, that bit of metal would have taken no additional value in Mr. Taggett's eyes. On leaving Mrs. Spooner's he held it tightly clasped in his fingers until he reached an unfrequented street, where he halted a moment in the shadow of a building to inspect the paper, which he had half forgotten in his satisfaction at having obtained the key. A stifled cry rose to Mr. Taggett's lips as he glanced over the crumpled note-sheet.

It contained three lines, hastily scrawled in lead-pencil, requesting Richard Shackford to call at the house in Welch's Court at eight o'clock on a certain Tuesday night. The note had been written, as the date showed, on the day preceding the Tuesday night in question - the night of the murder!

For a second or two Mr. Taggett stood paralyzed. Ten minutes afterwards a message in cipher was pulsing along the wires to New York, and before the sun went down that evening Richard Shackford was under the surveillance of the police.

The doubtful, unknown ground upon which Mr. Taggett had been floundering was now firm under his feet, - unexpected ground, but solid. Meeting Mary Hennessey in the street, on his way to the marble yard, Mr. Taggett no longer hesitated to accost her, and question her as to the story she had told William Durgin. The girl's story was undoubtedly true, and as a piece of circumstantial evidence was only less important than the elder Shackford's note. The two cousins had been for years on the worst of terms. At every step Mr. Taggett had found corroboration of Wollaston's statement to that effect.

"Where were Coroner Whidden's eyes and ears," wrote Mr. Taggett, - the words were dashed down impatiently on the page, as if he had sworn a little internally while writing them, - "when he conducted that inquest! In all my experience there was never a thing so stupidly managed."

A thorough and immediate examination of Richard Shackford's private workshop was now so imperative that Mr. Taggett resolved to make it even if he had to do so under the authority of a search-warrant. But he desired as yet to avoid publicity.

A secret visit to the studio seemed equally difficult by day and night. In the former case he was nearly certain to be deranged by the servants, and in the latter a light in the unoccupied room would alarm any of the household who might chance to awaken. From the watchman no danger was to be apprehended, as the windows of the extension were not visible from the street.

Mr. Taggett finally decided on the night as the more propitious time for his attempt, - a decision which his success justified. A brilliant moon favored the in-door part of the enterprise, though it exposed him to observation in his approach from the marble yard to the veranda.

With the dense moonlight streaming outside against the window-shades, he could safely have used a candle in the studio instead of the screened lantern which he had provided. Mr. Taggett passed three hours in the workshop, - the last hour in waiting for the moon to go down. Then he stole through the marble yard into the silent street, and hurried home, carrying two small articles concealed under his blouse. The first was a chisel with a triangular piece broken out of the centre of the bevel, and the other was a box of safety-matches. The peculiarity of this box of matches was - that just one match had been used from it.

Mr. Taggett's work was done.

The last seven pages of the diary were devoted to a review of the case, every detail of which was held up in various lights, and examined with the conscientious pains of a lapidary deciding on the value of a rare stone. The concluding entries ran as follow: -

"Tuesday Night. Here the case passes into other hands. I have been fortunate rather than skillful in unmasking the chief actor in one of the most singular crimes that ever came under my investigation. By destroying three objects, very easily destroyed, Richard Shackford would have put himself beyond the dream of suspicion. He neglected to remove these dumb witnesses, and now the dumb witnesses speak! If it could be shown that he was a hundred miles from Stillwater at the time of the murder, instead of in the village, as he was, he must still be held, in the face of the proofs against him, accessory to the deed. These proofs, roughly summarized, are: -

"First. The fact that he had had an altercation with his cousin a short time previous to the date of the murder, - a murder which may be regarded not as the result of a chance disagreement, but of long years of bitter enmity between the two men.

"Secondly. The fact that Richard Shackford had had an appointment with his cousin on the night the crime was committed, and had concealed that fact from the authorities at the time of the coroner's inquest.

"Thirdly. That the broken chisel found in the private workshop of the accused explains the peculiar shape of the wound which caused Lemuel Shackford's death, and corresponds in every particular with the plaster impression taken of that wound.

"Fourthly. That the partially consumed match found on

the scullery floor when the body was discovered (a style of match not used in the house in Welch's Court) completes the complement of a box of safety-matches belonging to Richard Shackford, and hidden in a closet in his workshop.

"Whether Shackford had an accomplice or not is yet to be ascertained. There is nothing whatever to implicate Mr. Rowland Slocum. I make the statement because his intimate association with one party and his deep dislike of the other invited inquiry, and at first raised an unjust suspicion in my mind."

The little red book slipped from Mr. Slocum's grasp and fell at his feet. As he rose from the chair, the reflection which he caught of himself in the dressing-table mirror was that of a wrinkled, white old man.

Mr. Slocum did not believe, and no human evidence could have convinced him, that Richard had deliberately killed Lemuel Shackford; but as Mr. Slocum reached the final pages of the diary, a horrible probability insinuated itself in his mind. Could Richard have done it accidentally? Could he - in an instant of passion, stung to sudden madness by that venomous old man - have struck him involuntarily, and killed him? A certain speech which Richard had made in Mr. Slocum's presence not long before came back to him now with fearful emphasis: -

"Three or four times in my life I have been carried away by a devil of a temper which I couldn't control, it seized me so unawares."

"It seized me so unawares!" repeated Mr. Slocum, half aloud; and then with a swift, unconscious gesture, he pressed his hands over his ears, as if to shut out the words.

XXI

Margaret must be told. It would be like stabbing her to tell her all this. Mr. Slocum had lain awake long after midnight, appalled by the calamity that was about to engulf them. At moments, as his thought reverted to Margaret's illness early in the spring, he felt that perhaps it would have been a mercy if she had died then. He had left the candles burning; it was not until the wicks sunk down in the sockets and went softly out that slumber fell upon him.

He was now sitting at the breakfast-table, absently crumbling bits of bread beside his plate and leaving his coffee untouched. Margaret glanced at him wistfully from time to time, and detected the restless night in the deepened lines of his face.

The house had not been the same since Lemuel Shackford's death; he had never crossed its threshold; Margaret had scarcely known him by sight, and Mr. Slocum had not spoken to him for years; but Richard's connection with the unfortunate old man had brought the tragic event very close to Margaret and her father. Mr. Slocum was a person easily depressed, but his depression this morning was so greatly in excess of the presumable cause that Margaret began to be troubled.

"Papa, has anything happened?"

"No, nothing new has happened; but I am dreadfully disturbed by some things which Mr. Taggett has been doing here in the village."

"I thought Mr. Taggett had gone."

"He did go; but he came back very quietly without anybody's knowledge. I knew it, of course; but no one else, to speak of."

"What has he done to disturb you?"

"I want you to be a brave girl, Margaret, - will you promise that?"

"Why, yes," said Margaret, with an anxious look. "You frighten me with your mysteriousness."

"I do not mean to be mysterious, but I don't quite know how to tell you about Mr. Taggett. He has been working underground in this matter of poor Shackford's death, - boring in the dark like a mole, - and thinks he has discovered some strange things."

"Do you mean he thinks he has found out whoi killed Mr. Shackford?"

"He believes he has fallen upon clews which will lead to that. The strange things I alluded to are things which Richard will have to explain."

"Richard? What has he to do with it?"

"Not much, I hope; but there are several matters which he will be obliged to clear up in order to save himself from very great annoyance. Mr. Taggett seems to think that - that" -

"Good heavens, papa! What does he think?"

"Margaret, he thinks that Richard knew something about the murder, and has not told it."

"What could he know? Is that all?"

"No, that is not all. I am keeping the full truth from you, and it is useless to do so. You must face it like a brave girl. Mr. Taggett suspects Richard of being concerned, directly or indirectly, with the crime."

The color went from Margaret's cheek for an instant. The statement was too horrible and sudden not to startle her, but it was also too absurd to have more than an instant's effect. Her quick recovery of herself reassured Mr. Slocum. Would she meet Mr. Taggett's specific charges with the like fortitude? Mr. Slocum himself had been prostrated by them; he prayed to Heaven that Margaret might have more strength than he, as indeed she had.

"The man has got together a lot of circumstantial evidence," continued Mr. Slocum cautiously; "some of it amounts to nothing, being mere conjecture; but some of it will look badly for Richard, to outsiders."

"Of course it is all a mistake," said Margaret, in nearly her natural voice. "It ought to be easy to convince Mr. Taggett of that."

"I have not been able to convince him."

"But you will. What has possessed him to fall into such

Thomas Bailey Aldrich

a ridiculous error?"

"Mr. Taggett has written out everything at length in this memorandum-book, and you must read it for yourself. There are expressions and statements in these pages, Margaret, that will necessarily shock you very much; but you should remember, as I tried to while reading them, that Mr. Taggett has a heart of steel; without it he would be unable to do his distressing work. The cold impartiality with which he sifts and heaps up circumstances involving the doom of a fellow-creature appears almost inhuman; but it is his business. No, don't look at it here!" said Mr. Slocum, recoiling; he had given the book to Margaret. "Take it into the other room, and read it carefully by yourself. When you have finished, come back and tell me what you think."

"But, papa, surely you" -

"I don't believe anything, Margaret! I don't know the true from the false any more! I want you to help me out of my confusion, and you cannot do it until you have read that book."

Margaret made no response, but passed into the parlor and closed the folding-doors behind her.

After an absence of half an hour she reentered the breakfast room, and laid Mr. Taggett's diary on the table beside her father, who had not moved from his place during the interval. Margaret's manner was collected, but it was evident, by the dark circles under her eyes, and the set, colorless lips, that that half hour had been a cruel thirty minutes to her. In Margaret's self-possession Mr. Slocum recognized, not for the first time, the cropping out of an ancestral trait which had somehow managed to avoid him in its wayward descent.

"Well?" he questioned, looking earnestly at Margaret, and catching a kind of comfort from her confident bearing.

"It is Mr. Taggett's trade to find somebody guilty," said Margaret, "and he has been very ingenious and very merciless. He was plainly at his wits' ends to sustain his reputation, and would not have hesitated to sacrifice any onen rather than wholly fail."

"But you have been crying, Margaret."

"How could I see Richard dragged down in the dust in this fashion, and not be mortified and indignant?"

"You don't believe anything at all of this?"

"Do *you?*" asked Margaret, looking through and through him.

"I confess I am troubled."

"If you doubt Richard for a second," said Margaret, with a slight quiver of her lip, "that will be the bitterest part of it to me."

"I don't give any more credit to Mr. Taggett's general charges than you do, Margaret; but I understand their gravity better. A perfectly guiltless man, one able with a single word to establish his innocence, is necessarily crushed at first by an accusation of this kind. Now, can Richard set these matters right with a single word? I am afraid he has a world of difficulty before him."

"When he returns he will explain everything. How can you question it?"

"I do not wish to; but there are two things in Mr. Taggett's story which stagger me. The motive for the destruction of Shackford's papers, - that's not plain; the box of matches is a puerility unworthy of a clever man like Mr. Taggett, and as to the chisel he found, why, there are a hundred broken chisels in the village, and probably a score of them broken in precisely the same manner; but, Margaret, did Richard every breathe a word to you of that quarrel with his cousin?"

"No."

"He never mentioned it to me either. As matters stood between you and him, nothing was more natural than that he should have spoken of it to you, - so natural that his silence is positively strange."

"He may have considered it too unimportant. Mr. Shackford always abused Richard; it was nothing new. Then, again, Richard is very proud, and perhaps he did not care to come to us just at that time with family grievances. Besides, how do we know they quarreled? The village is full of gossip."

"I am certain there was a quarrel; it was only necessary for those two to meet to insure that. I distinctly remember the forenoon when Richard went to Welch's Court; it was the day he discharged Torrini."

A little cloud passed over Margaret's countenance.

"They undoubtedly had angry words together," continued Mr. Slocum, "and we are forced to accept the Hennessey girl's statement. The reason you suggest for Richard's not saying anything on the subject may suffice for us, but it will scarcely satisfy disinterested persons, and doesn't at all cover another circumstance which must be taken in the same connection."

"What circumstance?"

"His silence in regard to Lemuel Shackford's note, - a note written the day before the murder, and making an appointment for the very night of it."

The girl looked steadily at her father.

"Margaret!" exclaimed Mr. Slocum, his face illuminated with a flickering hope as he met her untroubled gaze, "did Richard tell *you?*"

"No," replied Margaret.

"Then he told no one," said Mr. Slocum, with the light fading out of his features again. "It was madness in him to conceal the fact. He should not have lost a moment, after the death of his cousin, in making that letter public. It ought instantly to have been placed in Coroner Whidden's hands. Richard's action is inconceivable, unless - unless" -

"Do not say it!" cried Margaret. "I should never forgive you!"

In recapitulating the points of Mr. Taggett's accusation, Mr. Slocum had treated most of them as trivial; but he had not been sincere. He knew that that broken chisel had no duplicate in

Stillwater, and that the finding of it in Richard's closet was a black fact. Mr. Slocum had also glossed over the quarrel; but that letter! - the likelihood that Richard kept the appointment, and his absolute silence concerning it, - here was a grim thing which no sophistry could dispose of. It would be wronging Margaret to deceive her as to the vital seriousness of Richard's position.

"Why, why did he hide it!" Mr. Slocum persisted.

"I do not see that he really hid it, papa. He shut the note in a book lying openly on the table, - a dictionary, to which any one in the household was likely to go. You think Mr. Taggett a person of great acuteness."

"He is a very intelligent person, Margaret."

"He appears to me very short-sighted. If Richard were the dreadful man Mr. Taggett supposes, that paper would have been burnt, and not left for the first comer to pick up. I scorn myself for stooping to the suggestion!"

"There is something in the idea," said Mr. Slocum slowly. "But why did Richard never mention the note, - to you, or to me, or to anybody?"

"He had a sufficient reason, you may be sure. Oh, papa, how ready you are to believe evil of him!"

"I am not, God knows!"

"How you cling to this story of the letter! Suppose it

turns out to be some old letter, written two or three years ago? You could never look Richard in the face again."

"Unfortunately, Shackford dated it. It is useless for us to blindfold ourselves, Margaret. Richard has managed in some way to get himself into a very perilous situation, and we cannot help him by shutting our eyes. You misconceive me if you imagine I think him capable of coolly plotting his cousin's death; but it is not outside the limits of the possible that what has happened a thousand times may have happened once more. Men less impulsive than Richard" -

"I will not listen to it!" interrupted Margaret, drawing herself up. "When Richard returns he will explain the matter to you, - not to me. If I required a word of denial from him, I should care very little whether he was innocent or not."

Mr. Slocum threw a terrified glance at his daughter. Her lofty faith sent a chill to his heart. What would be the result of a fall from such a height? He almost wished Margaret had something less of that ancestral confidence and obstinacy the lack of which in his own composition he had so often deplored.

"We are not to speak of this to Richard," he said, after a protracted pause; "at least not until Mr. Taggett considers it best. I have pledged myself to something like that."

"Has Richard been informed of Mr. Taggett's singular proceeding?" asked Margaret, freezingly.

"Not yet; nothing is to be done until Mr. Taggett

returns from New York, and then Richard will at once have an opportunity of clearing himself."

"It would have spared us all much pain and misunderstanding if he had been sent for in the first instance. Did he know that this person was here in the yard?"

"The plan was talked over before Richard left; the details were arranged afterwards. He heartily approved of the plan."

A leisurely and not altogether saint-like smile crept into the corners of Margaret's mouth.

"Yes, he approved of the plan," repeated Mr. Slocum. "Perhaps he" - Here Mr. Slocum checked himself, and left the sentence flying at loose ends. Perhaps Richard had looked with favor upon a method of inquiry which was so likely to lead to no result. But Mr. Slocum did not venture to finish the suggestion. He had never seen Margaret so imperious and intractable; it was impossible to reason or to talk frankly with her. He remained silent, sitting with one arm thrown dejectedly across the back of the chair.

Presently his abject attitude and expression began to touch Margaret; there was something that appealed to her in the thin gray hair fallowing over his forehead. Her eyes softened as they rested upon him, and a pitying little tremor came to her under lip.

"Papa," she said, stooping to his side, with a sudden rosy bloom in her cheeks, "I have all the proof I want that Richard knew nothing of this dreadful business."

" You have proof!" exclaimed Mr. Slocum, starting

from his seat.

"Yes. The morning Richard went to New York" - Margaret hesitated.

"Well!"

"He put his arm around me and kissed me."

"Well!"

"Well?" repeated Margaret. "Could Richard have done that, - could he have so much as laid his hand upon me - if - if" -

Mr. Slocum sunk back in the chair with a kind of groan.

"Papa, you do not know him!"

"Oh, Margaret, I am afraid that that is not the kind of evidence to clear Richard in Mr. Taggett's eyes."

"Then Richard's word must do it," she said haughtily. "He will be home to-night."

"Yes, he is to return to-night," said Mr. Slocum, looking away from her.

XXII

During the rest of the day the name of Richard Shackford was not mentioned again by either Margaret or her father. It was a day of suspense to both, and long before night-fall Margaret's impatience for Richard to come had resolved itself into a pain as keen as that with which Mr. Slocum contemplated the coming; for every hour augmented his dread of the events that would necessarily follow the reappearance of young Shackford in Stillwater.

On reaching his office, after the conversation with Margaret, Mr. Slocum found Lawyer Perkins waiting for him. Lawyer Perkins, who was as yet in ignorance of the late developments, had brought information of his own. The mutilated document which had so grimly clung to its secret was at last deciphered. It proved to be a recently executed will, in which the greater part of Lemuel Shackford's estate, real and personal, was left unconditionally to his cousin.

"That disposes of one of Mr. Taggett's theories," was Mr. Slocum's unspoken reflection. Certainly Richard had not destroyed the will; the old man himself had destroyed it, probably in some fit of pique. Yet, after all, the vital question was in no way affected by this fact; the motive for the crime remained, and the fearful evidence against Richard still held.

After the departure of Lawyer Perkins, who had been struck by the singular perturbation of his old friend, Mr. Slocum drew forth Mt. Taggett's journal, and re-read it from beginning to end. Margaret's unquestioning faith in Richard, her prompt and indignant rejection of the whole story, had shaken her father at moments that morning; but now his paralyzing doubts returned. This second perusal of the diary impressed him even more strongly than the first. Richard had killed Lemuel Shackford, - in self-defense, may be, or perhaps accidentally; but he had killed him! As Mr. Slocum passed from page to page, following the dark thread of narrative that darkened at each remove, he lapsed into that illogical frame of mind when one looks half expectantly for some providential interposition to avert the calamity against which human means are impotent. If Richard were to drop dead in the street! If he were to fall overboard off Point Judith in the night! If only anything would happen to prevent his coming back! Thus the ultimate disgrace might be spared them. But the ill thing is the sure thing; the letter with the black seal never miscarries, and Richard was bound to come! "There is no escape for him or for us," murmured Mr. Slocum, closing his finger in the book.

It was in a different mood that Margaret said to herself, "It is nearly four o'clock; he will be here at eight!" As she stood at the parlor window and watched the waning afternoon light making its farewells to the flower-beds in the little square front-gardens of the houses opposite, Margaret's heart was filled with the tenderness of the greeting she intended to give Richard. She had never been cold or shy in her demeanor with him, nor had she ever been quite demonstrative; but now she meant to put her arms around his neck in a wifely fashion, and recompense him so far as she could for all the injustice he was to suffer. When he came to learn of the hateful slander that had lifted its head during his absence, he should already be in possession of the assurance of her faith.

In the mean while the hands in Slocum's Yard were much exercised over the unaccountable disappearance of Blake. Stevens reported the matter to Mr. Slocum.

"Ah, yes," said Mr. Slocum, who had not provided himself with an explanation, and was puzzled to improvise one. "I discharged him, - that is to say, I let him go. I forgot to mention it. He didn't take to the trade."

"But he showed a good fist for a beginner," said Stevens. "He was head and shoulders the best of the new lot. Shall I put Stebbins in his place?"

"You needn't do anything until Mr. Shackford gets back."

"When will that be, sir?"

"To-night, probably."

The unceremonious departure of Blake formed the theme of endless speculation at the tavern that evening, and for the moment obscured the general interest in old Shackford's murder.

"Never to let on he was goin'!" said one.

"Didn't say good-by to nobody," remarked a second.

"It was devilish uncivil," added a third.

"It is kind of mysterious," said Mr. Peters.

"Some girl," suggested Mr. Willson, with an air of tender sentiment, which he attempted further to emphasize by a capricious wink.

"No," observed Dexter. "When a man vanishes in that sudden way his body is generally found in a clump of blackberry bushes, months afterwards, or left somewhere on the flats by an ebb tide."

"Two murders in Stillwater in one month would be rather crowding it, wouldn't it?" inquired Piggott.

"Bosh!" said Durgin. "There was always something shady about Blake. We didn't know where he hailed from, and we don't know where he's gone to. He'll take care of himself; that kind of fellow never lets anybody play any points on him." With this Durgin threw away the stump of his cigar, and lounged out at the street door.

"I couldn't get anything out of the proprietor," said Stevens; "but he never talks. May be Shackford when he" - Stevens stopped short to listen to a low, rumbling sound like distant thunder, followed almost instantly by two quick faint whistles. "He's aboard the train to-night."

Mr. Peters quietly rose from his seat and left the bar-room.

The evening express, due at eight, was only a few seconds behind time. As the screech of the approaching engine rung out from the dark wood-land, Margaret and her father exchanged rapid glances. It would take Richard ten minutes to walk from the railway station to the house, - for of course he would come there directly after sending his valise to Lime Street.

The ten minutes went by, and then twenty. Margaret bent steadily over her work, listening with covert intentness for the click of the street gate. Likely enough Richard had been unable to find any one to take charge of his hand-baggage. Presently Mr. Slocum could not resist the impulse to look at his watch. It was half past eight. He nervously unfolded The Stillwater Gazette, and sat with his eyes fastened on the paper.

After a seemingly interminable period the heavy bell of the South Church sounded nine, and then tolled for a few minutes, as the dismal custom is in New England country towns.

A long silence followed, unrelieved by any word between father and daughter, - a silence so profound that the heart of the old-fashioned time-piece, throbbing monotonously in its dusky case at the foot of the stairs, made itself audible through the room. Mr. Slocum's gaze continued fixed on the newspaper which he was not reading. Margaret's hands lay crossed over the work on her lap.

Ten o'clock.

"What can have kept him?" murmured Margaret.

"There was only that way out of it," reflected Mr. Slocum, pursuing his own line of thought.

Margaret's cheeks were flushed and hot, and her eyes

dulled with disappointment, as she rose from the low rocking-chair and crossed over to kiss her father good-night. Mr. Slocum drew the girl gently towards him, and held her for a moment in silence. But Margaret, detecting the subtile commiseration in his manner, resented it, and released herself coldly.

"He has been detained, papa."

"Yes, something must have detained him!"

XXIII

When the down express arrived at Stillwater, that night, two passengers stepped from the rear car to the platform: one was Richard Shackford, and the other a commercial traveler, whose acquaintance Richard had made the previous evening on the Fall River boat.

There were no hacks in waiting at the station, and Richard found his politeness put to a severe test when he saw himself obliged to pilot his companion part of the way to the hotel, which lay - it seemed almost maliciously - in a section of the town remote from the Slocums'. Curbing his impatience, Richard led the stranger through several crooked, unlighted streets, and finally left him at the corner of the main thoroughfare, within pistol-shot of the red glass lantern which hung over the door of the tavern. This cost Richard ten good minutes. As he hurriedly turned into a cross-street on the left, he fancied that he heard his name called several times from somewhere in the darkness. A man came running towards him. It was Mr. Peters.

"Can I say a word to you, Mr. Shackford?"

"If it isn't a long one. I am rather pressed."

"It is about Torrini, sir."

"What of him?"

"He's mighty bad, sir."

"Oh, I can't stop to hear that," and Richard quickened his pace.

"The doctor took off his hand last Wednesday," said Peters, keeping alongside, "and he's been getting worse and worse."

Richard halted. "Took off his hand?"

"Didn't you know he was caught in the rolling-machine at Dana's? Well, it was after you went away."

"This is the first I've heard of it."

"It was hard lines for him, sir, with the woman and the two children, and nothing to eat in the house. The boys in the yard have done what they could, but with the things from the drug-store, and so on, we couldn't hold up our end. Mr. Dana paid the doctor's bill, but if it hadn't been for Miss Slocum I don't know what would have happened. I thought may be if I spoke to you, and told you how it was" -

"Did Torrini send you?"

"Lord, no! He's too proud to send to anybody. He's been so proud since they took off his hand that there has been no doing anything with him. If they was to take off his leg, he would turn into one mass of pride. No, Mr. Shackford, I came of myself."

"Where does Torrini live, now?"

"In Mitchell's Alley."

"I will go along with you," said Richard, with a dogged air. It seemed as if the fates were determined to keep him from seeing Margaret that night. Peters reached out a hand to take Richard's leather bag. "No, thank you, I can carry it very well." In a small morocco case in one of the pockets was a heavy plain gold ring for Margaret, and not for anything in the world would Richard have allowed any one else to carry the bag.

After a brisk five minutes' walk the two emerged upon a broad street crossing their path at right angles. All the shops were closed except Stubbs the provision dealer's and Dundon's drug-store. In the window of the apothecary a great purple jar, with a spray of gas jets behind it, was flaring on the darkness like a Bengal light. Richard stopped at the provision store and made some purchases; a little further on he halted at a fruit stand, kept by an old crone, who had supplemented the feeble flicker of the corner street lamp with a pitch-pine torch, which cast a yellow bloom over her apples and turned them all into oranges. She had real oranges, however, and Richard selected half a dozen, with a confused idea of providing the little Italians with some national fruit, though both children had been born in Stillwater.

Then the pair resumed their way, Peters acting as pioneer. They soon passed beyond the region of sidewalks and curbstones, and began picking their steps through a narrow, humid lane, where the water lay in slimy pools, and the tenement houses on each side blotted out the faint starlight. The night was sultry, and door and casement stood wide, making pits of darkness. Few lights were visible, but a continuous hum of voices issued from the human hives, and now and then a transient red glow at an upper window showed that some one was smoking a pipe. This was Mitchell's Alley.

The shadows closed behind the two men as they moved forward, and neither was aware of the figure which had been discreetly following them for the last ten minutes. If Richard had suddenly wheeled and gone back a dozen paces, he would have come face to face with the commercial traveler.

Mr. Peeters paused in front of one of the tenement houses, and motioned with his thumb over his shoulder for Richard to follow him through a yawning doorway. The hall was as dark as a cave, and full of stale, moldy odors. Peters shuffled cautiously along the bare boards until he kicked his toe against the first step of the staircase.

"Keep close to the wall, Mr. Shackford, and feel your way up. They've used the banisters for kindling, and the landlord says he shan't put in any more. I went over here the other night," added Mr. Peters reminiscentially.

After fumbling several seconds for the latch, Mr. Peters pushed open a door, and ushered Richard into a large, gloomy rear room. A kerosene lamp was burning dimly on the mantel-shelf, over which hung a coarsely-colored lithograph of the Virgin in a pine frame. Under the picture stood a small black crucifix. There was little furniture, - a cooking-stove, two or three stools, a broken table, and a chest of drawers. On an iron bedstead in the corner lay Torrini, muffled to the chin in a blanket, despite the hot midsummer night. His right arm, as if it were wholly disconnected with his body, rested in a splint on the outside of the covering. As the visitors entered, a tall dusky woman with blurred eyes rose from a low bench at the foot of the bed.

"Is he awake?" asked Peters.

The woman, comprehending the glance which accompanied the words, though not the words themselves, nodded yes.

"Here is Mr. Shackford come to see you, Torrini," Peters said.

The man slowly unclosed his eyes; they were unnaturally brilliant and dilated, and seemed to absorb the rest of his features.

"I didn't want him."

"Let by-gones be by-gones, Torrini," said Richard, approaching the bedside. "I am sorry about this."

"You are very good; I don't understand. I ask nothing of Slocum; but the signorina comes every day, and I cannot help it. What would you have? I'm a dead man," and he turned away his face.

"It is not so bad as that," said Richard.

Torrini looked up with a ghastly smile. "They have cut off the hand that struck you, Mr. Shackford."

"I suppose it was necessary. I am very sorry. In a little while you will be on your feet again."

"It is too late. They might have saved me by taking the arm, but I would not allow them. I may last three or four days. The doctor says it."

Peters, standing in the shadow, jerked his head affirmatively.

"I do not care for myself," the man continued, - "but she and the little ones - That is what madden s me. They will starve."

"They will not be let starve in Stillwater," said Richard.

Torrini turned his eyes upon him wistfully and doubtfully. "You will help them?"

"Yes, I and others."

"If they could be got to Italy," said Torrini, after meditating, "it would be well. Her farther," giving a side look at the woman, "is a fisherman of Capri." At the word Capri the woman lifted her head quickly. "He is not rich, but he's not poor; he would take her."

"You would wish her sent to Naples?"

"Yes."

"If you do not pull through, she and the children shall go there."

"Brigida!" called Torrini; then he said something rapidly in Italian to the woman, who buried her face in both hands, and did not reply.

"She has no words to thank you. See, she is tired to death, with the children all day and me all night, - these many nights."

"Tell her to go to bed in the other room," said Richard. "There's another room, isn't there? I'll sit with you."

"You?"

"Your wife is fagged out, - that is plain. Send her to bed, and don't talk any more. Peters, I wish you'd run and get a piece of ice somewhere; there's no drinking-water here. Come, now, Torrini, I can't speak Italian. Oh, I don't mind your scowling; I intend to stay."

Torrini slowly unknitted his brows, and an irresolute expression stole across his face; then he called Brigida, and bade her go in with the children. She bowed her head submissively, and fixing her melting eyes on Richard for an instant passed into the adjoining chamber.

Peters shortly reappeared with the ice, and after setting a jug of water on the table departed. Richard turned up the wick of the kerosene lamp, which was sending forth a disagreeable odor, and pinned an old newspaper around the chimney to screen the flame. He had, by an odd chance, made his lampshade out of a copy of The Stillwater Gazette containing the announcement of his cousin's death. Richard gave a quick start as his eye caught the illuminated head-lines, - Mysterious Murder of Lemuel Shackford! Perhaps a slight exclamation escaped Richard's lips at the same time, for Torrini turned and asked what was the matter. "Nothing at all," said Richard, removing the paper, and placing another in its stead. Then he threw open the blinds of the window looking on the back yard, and set his hand-bag against the door to prevent it being blown to by the draught. Torrini, without altering the rigid position of his head on the pillow, followed every movement with a look of curious insistence, like that of the eyes in a portrait. His preparations completed for the night, Richard seated himself on a stool at the foot of the bed.

The obscurity and stillness of the room had their effect upon the sick man, who presently dropped into a light sleep. Richard sat thinking of Margaret, and began to be troubled because he had neglected to send her word of his detention, which he might have done by Peters. It was now too 1 ate. The town clock struck ten in the midst of his self-reproaches. At the first clang of the bell, Torrini awoke with a start, and asked for water.

"If anybody comes," he said, glancing in a bewildered, anxious way at the shadows huddled about the door, "you are not to leave me alone with him."

"Him? Whom? Are you expecting any one?"

"No; but who knows? one might come. Then, you are not to go; you are not to leave me for a second."

"I've no thought of it," replied Richard; "you may rest easy.... He's a trifle light in the head," was Richard's reflection.

After that Torrini dozed rather than slumbered, rousing at brief intervals; and whenever he awoke the feverish activity of his brain incited him to talk, - nowe of Italy, and now of matters connected with his experiences in this country.

Thomas Bailey Aldrich

"Naples is a pleasant place!" he broke out in the hush of the midnight, just as Richard was dropping off. "The band plays every afternoon on the Chiaia. And then the *festas,* - every third day a festa. The devil was in my body when I left there and dragged little Brigida into all this misery. We used to walk of an evening along the Marinella, - that's a strip of beach just beyond the Molo Piccolo. You were never in Naples?"

"Not I," said Richard. "Here, wet your lips, and try to go to sleep again."

"No, I can't sleep for thinking. When the Signorina came to see me, the other day, her heart was pierced with pity. Like the blessed Madonna's, her bosom bleeds for all! You will let her come to-morrow?"

"Yes, yes! If you will only keep quiet, Margaret shall come."

"Margherita, we say. You are to we her, - is it nnot so?"

Richard turned down the wick of the lamp, which was blazing and spluttering, and did not answer. Then Torrini lay silent a long while, apparently listening to the hum of the telegraph wires attached to one end of the roof. At odd intervals the freshening breeze swept these wires, and awoke a low æolian murmur. The moon rose in the mean time, and painted on the uncarpeted floor the shape of the cherry bough that stretched across the window. It was two o'clock; Richard sat with his head bent forward, in a drowse.

"Now the cousin is dead, you are as rich as a prince, - are you not?" inquired Torrini, who had lain for the last half hour with his eyes wide open in the moonlight.

Richard straightened himself with a jerk.

"Torrini, I positively forbid you to talk any more!"

"I remember you said that one day, somewhere. Where was it? Ah, in the yard! 'You can't be allowed to speak here, you know.' And then I struck at you, - with that hand they've taken away! See how I remember it!"

"Why do you bother your mind with such things? Think of just nothing at all, and rest. Perhaps a wet cloth on your forehead will refresh you. I wish you had a little of my genius for not keeping awake."

"You are tired, you?"

"I have had two broken nights, traveling."

"And I give you no peace?"

"Well, no," returned Richard bluntly, hoping the admission would induce Torrini to tranquilize himself, "you don't give me much."

"Has any one been here?" demanded Torrini abruptly.

"Not a soul. Good Heaven, man, do you know what time it is?"

"I know, - I know. It's very late. I ought to keep quiet; but, the devil! with this fever in my brain! . . . . Mr. Shackford!" and Torrini, in spite of his imprisoned limb, suddenly half raised himself from the mattress.

"I - I" -

Richard sprung to his feet. "What is it, - what do you want?"

"Nothing," said Torrini, falling back on the pillow.

Richard brought him a glass of water, which he refused. He lay motionless, with his eyes shut, as if composing himself, and Richard returned on tiptoe to his bench. A moment or two afterwards Torrini stirred the blanket with his foot.

"Mr. Shackford!"

"Well?"

"I am as grateful - as a dog."

Torrini did not speak again. This expression of his gratitude appeared to ease him. His respiration grew lighter and more regular, and by and by he fell into a profound sleep. Richard watched awhile expectantly, with his head resting against the rail of the bedstead; then his eyelids drooped, and he too slumbered. But once or twice, before he quite lost himself, he was conscious of Brigida's thin face thrust like a silver wedge through the half-open door of the hall bedroom. It was the last thing he remembered, - that sharp, pale face peering out from the blackness of the inner chamber as his grasp loosened on the world and he drifted off on the tide of a dream. A narrow white hand, like a child's, seemed to be laid against his breast. It was not Margaret's hand, and yet it was hers. No, it was the plaster model he had made that idle summer afternoon, years and years before he had ever thought of loving her. Strange for it to be there! Then Richard began wondering how the gold ring would look in the slender forefinger. He unfastened the leather bag and took out the ring. He was vainly trying to pass it over the first joint of the dead white finger, when the cast slipped from his hold and fell with a crash to the floor. Richard gave a shudder, and opened his eyes. Brigida was noiselessly approaching Torrini's bedside. Torrini still slept. It was broad day. Through the uncurtained window Richard saw the blue sky barred with crimson.

XXIV

"Richard did come home last night, after all," said Mr. Slocum, with a flustered air, seating himself at the breakfast table.

Margaret looked up quickly.

"I just met Peters on the street, and he told me," added Mr. Slocum.

"Richard returned last night, and did not come to us!"

"It seems that he watched with Torrini, - the man is going to die."

"Oh," said Margaret, cooling instantly. "That was like Richard; he never thinks of himself first. I would not have had him do differently. Last evening you were filled with I don't know what horrible suspicions, yet see how simply everything explains itself."

"If I could speak candidly, Margaret, if I could express myself without putting you into a passion, I would tell you that Richard's passing the night with that man has given me two or three ugly ideas."

"Positively, papa, you are worse than Mr. Taggett."

"I shall not say another word," replied Mr. Slocum. Then he unfolded the newspaper lying beside him, and constructed a barrier against further colloquy.

An hour afterwards, when Richard threw open the door of his private workshop, Margaret was standing in the middle of the room waiting for him. She turned with a little cry of pleasure, and allowed Richard to take her in his arms, and kept to the spirit and the letter of the promise she had made to herself. If there was an unwonted gravity in Margaret's manner, young Shackford was not keen enough to perceive it. All that morning, wherever he went, he carried with him a sense of Margaret's face resting for a moment against his shoulder, and the happiness of it rendered him wholly oblivious to the constrained and chilly demeanor of her father when they met. The interview was purposely cut short by Mr. Slocum, who avoided Richard the rest of the day with a persistency that must have ended in forcing itself upon his notice, had he not been so engrossed by the work which had accumulated during his absence.

Mr. Slocum had let the correspondence go to the winds, and a formidable collection of unanswered letters lay on Shackford's desk. The forenoon was consumed in reducing the pile and settling the questions that had risen in the shops, for Mr. Slocum had neglected everything. Richard was speedily advised of Blake's dismissal from the yard, but, not knowing what explanation had been offered, was unable to satisfy Stevens' curiosity on the subject. "I must see Slocum about that at once," reflected Richard; but the opportunity did not occur, and he was too much pressed to make a special business of it.

Mr. Slocum, meanwhile, was in a wretched state of suspense and apprehension. Justice Beemis's clerk had served some sort of legal paper - presumably a subpoena - on Richard, who had coolly read it in the yard under the gaze of all, and given no sign of discomposure beyond a momentary lifting of the eyebrows. Then he had carelessly thrust the paper into one of his pockets and continued his directions to the men. Clearly he had as yet no suspicion of the mine that was ready to be sprung under his feet.

Shortly after this little incident, which Mr. Slocum had witnessed from the window of the counting-room, Richard spoke a word or two to Stevens, and quitted the yard. Mr. Slocum dropped into the carving department.

"Where is Mr. Shackford, Stevens?"

"He has gone to Mitchell's Alley, sir. Said he'd be away an hour. Am I to say he was wanted?"

"No," replied Mr. Slocum, hastily; "any time will do. You needn't mention that I inquired for him," and Mr. Slocum returned to the counting-room.

Before the hour expired he again distinguished Richard's voice in the workshops, and the cheery tone of it was a positive affront to Mr. Slocum. Looking back to the week prior to the tragedy in Welch's Court, he recollected Richard's unaccountable dejection; he had had the air of a person meditating some momentous step, - the pallor, the set face, and the introspective eyes. Then came the murder, and Richard's complete prostration. Mr. Slocum in his own excitement had noted it superficially at the time, but now he recalled the young man's inordinate sorrow, and it seemed rather like remorse. Was his present immobile serenity the natural expression of a man whose heart had suddenly ossified, and was no longer capable of throbbing with its guilt? Richard Shackford was rapidly becoming an awful problem to Mr. Slocum.

Since the death of his cousin, Richard had not been so much like his former self. He appeared to have taken up his cheerfulness at the point where he had dropped it three weeks before. If there were any weight resting on his mind, he bore it lightly, with a kind of careless defiance.

In his visit that forenoon to Mitchell's Alley he had arranged for Mrs. Morganson, his cousin's old house-keeper, to watch with Torrini the ensuing night. This left Richard at liberty to spend the evening with Margaret, and finish his correspondence. Directly after tea he repaired to the studio, and, lighting the German student-lamp, fell to work on the letters. Margaret came in shortly with a magazine, and seated herself near the round table at which he was writing. She had dreaded this evening; it could scarcely pass without some mention of Mr. Taggett, and she had resolved not to speak of him. If Richard questioned her it would be very distressing. How could she tell Richard that Mr. Taggett accused him of the murder of his cousin, and that her own father half believed the accusation? No, she could never acknowledge that.

For nearly an hour the silence of the room was interrupted only by the scratching of Richard's pen and the rustling of the magazine as Margaret turned the leaf. Now and then he looked up and caught her eye, and smiled, and went on with his task. It was a veritable return of the old times. Margaret became absorbed in the story she was reading and forgot her uneasiness. Her left hand rested on the pile of answered letters, to which Richard added one at intervals, she mechanically lifting her palm and replacing it on the fresh manuscript. Presently Richard observed this movement and smiled in secret at the slim white hand unconsciously making a paper-weight of itself. He regarded it covertly for a moment, and then his disastrous dream occurred to him. There should be no mistake this time. He drew the small morocco case from his pocket, and leaning across the table slipped the ring on Margaret's finger.

Margaret gave a bewildered start, and then seeing what Richard had done held out her hand to him with a gracious, impetuous little gesture.

"I mean to give it you this morning," he said, pressing his lip to the ring, "but the daylight did not seem fine enough for it."

"I thought you had forgotten," said Margaret, slowly turning the band on her finger.

"The first thing I did in New York was to go to a jeweler's for this ring, and since then I have guarded it day and night as dragonishly as if it had been the Koh-i-Noor diamond, or some inestimable gem which hundreds of envious persons were lying in wait to wrest from me. Walking the streets with this trinket in my possession, I have actually had a sense of personal insecurity. I seemed to invite general assault. That was being very sentimental, was it not?"

"Yes, perhaps."

"That small piece of gold meant so much to me."

"And to me," said Margaret. "Have you finished your letters?"

"Not yet. I shall be through in ten minutes, and then we'll have the evening to ourselves."

Richard hurriedly resumed his writing and Margaret turned to her novel again; but the interest had faded out of it; the figures had grown threadbare and indistinct, like the figures in a piece of old tapestry, and after a moment or two the magazine glided with an unnoticed flutter into the girl's lap. She sat absently twirling the gold loop on her finger.

Richard added the address to the final envelope, dried it with the blotter, and abruptly shut down the lid of the inkstand with an air of as great satisfaction as if he had been the fisherman in the Arabian story corking up the wicked afrite. With his finger still pressing the leaden cover, as though he were afraid the imp of toil would get out again, he was suddenly impressed by the fact that he had seen very little of Mr. Slocum that day.

"I have hardly spoken to him," he reflected. "Where is your father, to-night?"

"He has a headache," said Margaret. "He went to his room immediately after supper."

"It is nothing serious, of course."

"I fancy not; papa is easily excited, and he had had a

great deal to trouble him lately, - the strike, and all that."

"I wonder if Mr. Taggett has been bothering him."

"I dare say Mr. Taggett has bothered him."

"You knew of his being in the yard?"

"Not while he was here. Papa told me yesterday. I think Mr. Taggett was scarcely the person to render much assistance."

"Then he has found nothing whatever?"

"Nothing important."

"But anything? Trifles are of importance in a matter like this. Your father never wrote me a word about Taggett."

"Mr. Taggett has made a failure of it, Richard."

"If nothing new has transpired, then I do not under-stand the summons I received to-day."

"A summons!"

"I've the paper somewhere. No, it is in the pocket of my other coat. I take it there is to be a consultation of some kind at Justice Beemis's office to-morrow."

"I am very glad," said Margaret, with her face brightening. To-morrow would lift the cloud which had spread itself over them all, and was pressing down so heavily on one unconscious head. To-morrow

Richard's innocence should shine forth and confound Mr. Taggett. A vague bitterness rose in Margaret's heart as she thought of her father. "Let us talk of something else," she said, brusquely breaking her pause; "let us talk of something pleasant."

"Of ourselves, then," suggested Richard, banishing the shadow which had gathered in his eyes at his first mention of Mr. Taggett's name.

"Of ourselves," repeated Margaret gayly.

"Then you must give me your hand," stipulated Richard, drawing his chair closer to hers.

"There!" said Margaret.

While this was passing, Mr. Slocum, in the solitude of his chamber, was vainly attempting to solve the question whether he had not disregarded all the dictates of duty and common sense in allowing Margaret to spend the evening alone with Richard Shackford. Mr. Slocum saw one thing with painful distinctness - that he could not help himself.

XXV

The next morning Mr. Slocum did not make his appearance in the marble yard. His half-simulated indisposition of the previous night had turned into a genuine headache, of which he perhaps willingly availed himself to remain in his room, for he had no desire to see Richard Shackford that day.

It was an hour before noon. Up to that moment Richard had been engaged in reading and replying to the letters received by the morning's mail, a duty which usually fell to Mr. Slocum. As Richard stepped from the office into the yard a small boy thrust a note into his hand, and then stood off a short distance tranquilly boring with one toe in the loose gravel, and apparently waiting for an answer. Shackford hastily ran his eye over the paper, and turning towards the boy said, a little impatiently:

"Tell him I will come at once."

There was another person in Stillwater that forenoon whose agitation was scarcely less than Mr. Slocum's, though it greatly differed from it in quality. Mr. Slocum was alive to his finger-tips with dismay; Lawyer Perkins was boiling over with indignation. It was a complex indignation, in which astonishment and incredulity were nicely blended with a cordial detestation of Mr. Taggett and vague promptings to inflict some physical injury on Justice Beemis. That he, Melanchthon Perkins, the confidential legal adviser and personal friend of the late Lemuel Shackford, should have been kept for two weeks in profound ignorance of proceedings so nearly touching his lamented client! The explosion of the old lawyer's wrath was so unexpected that Justice Beemis, who had dropped in to make the disclosures and talk the matter over informally, clutched at his broad-brimmed Panama hat and precipitately retreated from the office. Mr. Perkins walked up and down the worn green drugget of his private room for half an hour afterwards, collecting himself, and then dispatched a hurried note to Richard Shackford, requesting an instant interview with him at his, Lawyer Perkins's, chambers.

When, some ten minutes subsequently, Richard entered the low-studded square room, darkened with faded moreen curtains and filled with a stale odor of law-calf, Mr. Perkins was seated at his desk and engaged in transferring certain imposing red-sealed documents to a green baize satchel which he held between his knees. He had regained his equanimity; his features wore their usual expression of judicial severity; nothing denoted his recent discomposure, except perhaps an additional wantonness in the stringy black hair falling over the high forehead, - that pallid high forehead which always wore the look of being covered with cold perspiration.

"Mr. Shackford," said Lawyer Perkins, suspending his operations a second, as he saluted the young man, "I suppose I have done an irregular thing in sending for you, but I did not see any other course open to me. I have been your cousin's attorney for over twenty-five years, and I've a great regard for you personally. That must justify the step I am taking."

"The regard is mutual, I am sure," returned Richard, rather surprised by this friendly overture, for his acquaintance with the lawyer had been of the slightest, though it had extended over many years. "My cousin had very few friends, and I earnestly desire to have them mine. If I were in any trouble, there is no one to whom I would come as unhesitatingly as to you."

"But you are in trouble."

"Yes, my cousin's death was very distressing."

"I do not mean that." Mr. Perkins paused a full moment. "The district attorney has suddenly taken a deep interest in the case, and there is to be a rigorous overhauling of the facts. I am afraid it is going to be very unpleasant for you, Mr. Shackford."

"How could it be otherwise?" asked Richard, tranquilly.

Lawyer Perkins fixed his black eyes on him. "Then you fully understand the situation, and can explain everything?"

"I wish I could. Unfortunately, I can explain nothing. I don't clearly see why I have been summoned to attend as a witness at the investigation to be held to-day in Justice Beemis's office."

"You are unacquainted with any special reason why your testimony is wanted?"

"I cannot conceive why it should be required. I gave my evidence at the time of the inquest, and have nothing to add to it. Strictly speaking, I have had of late years no relations with my cousin. During the last eighteen months we have spoken together but once."

"Have you had any conversation on this subject with Mr. Slocum since your return from New York?"

"No, I have had no opportunity. I was busy all day yesterday; he was ill in the evening, and is still confined to his room."

Mr. Perkins was manifestly embarrassed.

"That is unfortunate," he said, laying the bag on the desk. "I wish you had talked with Mr. Slocum. Of course you were taken into the secret of Taggett's presence in the marble yard?"

"Oh, yes; that was all arranged before I left home."

"You don't know the results of that manoeuvre?"

"There were no results."

"On the contrary, Taggett claims to have made very important discoveries."

"Indeed! Why was I not told!"

"I can't quite comprehend Mr. Slocum's silence."

"What has Taggett discovered?"

"Several things , upon which he builds the

Thomas Bailey Aldrich

gravest suspicions."

"Against whom?"

"Against you."

"Against me!" cried Richard, recoiling. The action was one altogether of natural amazement, and convinced Mr. Perkins, who had keenly watched the effect of his announcement, that young Shackford was being very hardly used.

Justice Beemis had given Mr. Perkins only a brief outline of the facts, and had barely touched on details when the old lawyer's anger had put an end to the conversation. His disgust at having been left out in the cold, though he was in no professional way concerned in the task of discovering the murderer of Lemuel Shackford, had caused Lawyer Perkins instantly to repudiate Mr. Taggett's action. "Taggett is a low, intriguing fellow," he had said to Justice Beemis; "Taggett is a fraud." Young Shackford's ingenuous manner now confirmed Mr. Perkins in that belief.

Richard recovered himself in a second or two. "Why did not Mr. Slocum mention these suspicions to me?" he demanded.

"Perhaps he found it difficult to do so."

"Why should he find it difficult?"

"Suppose he believed them."

"But he could not believe them, whatever they are."

"Well, then, suppose he was not at liberty to speak."

"It seems that you are, Mr. Perkins, and you owe it to me to be explicit. What does Taggett suspect?"

Lawyer Perkins brooded a while before replying. His practice was of a miscellaneous sort, confined in the main to what is technically termed office practice. Though he was frequently engaged in small cases of assault and battery, - he could scarcely escape that in Stillwater, - he had never conducted an important criminal case; but when Lawyer Perkins looked up from his brief reverie, he had fully resolved to undertake the defense of Richard Shackford.

"I will tell you what Taggett suspects," he said slowly, "if you will allow me to tell you in my own way. I must ask a number of questions."

Richard gave a half-impatient nod of assent.

"Where were you on the night of the murder?" inquired Lawyer Perkins, after a slight pause.

"I spent the evening at the Slocums', until ten o'clock; then I went home, - but not directly. It was moonlight, and I walked about, perhaps for an hour."

"Did you meet any one?"

"Not that I recollect. I walked out of town, on the turnpike."

"When you returned to your boarding-house, did you meet any one?"

"No, I let myself in with a pass-key. The family had retired, with the exception of Mr. Pinkham."

"Then you saw him?"

"No, but I heard him; he was playing on the flute at his chamber window, or near it. He always plays on the flute when he can't sleep."

"What o'clock was that?"

"It must have been after eleven."

"Your stroll was confined to the end of the town most remote from Welch's Court?"

"Yes, I just cruised around on the outskirts."

"I wish you had spoken with somebody that night."

"The streets were deserted. I wasn't likely to meet persons on the turnpike."

"However, some one may have seen you without your knowing it?"

"Yes," said Richard curtly. He was growing restive under these interrogations, the drift of which was plain enough to be disagreeable. Moreover, Mr. Perkins had insensibly assumed the tone and air of a counsel cross-examining a witness on the other side. This nocturnal cruise, whose direction and duration were known only to young Shackford, struck Lawyer Perkins unpleasantly. He meditated a moment before putting the next question.

"Were you on good terms - I mean fairly good terms - with your cousin?"

"No," said Richard; "but the fault was not mine. He never liked me. As a child I annoyed him, I suppose, and when I grew up I offended him by running away to sea. My mortal offense, however, was accepting a situation in Slocum's Yard. I have been in my cousin's house only twice in three years."

"When was the last time?"

"A day or two previous to the strike."

"As you were not in the habit of visiting the house, you must have had some purpose in going there. What was the occasion?"

Richard hung his head thoughtfully. "I went there to talk over family matters, - to inform him of my intended marriage to Margaret Slocum. I wanted his good-will and support. Mr. Slocum had offered to take me into the business. I thought perhaps my cousin Lemuel, seeing how prosperous I was, would be more friendly to me."

"Did you wish him to lend you capital?"

"I didn't expect or wish him to; but there was some question of that."

"And he refused?"

"Rather brutally, if I may say so now."

"Was there a quarrel?"

Thomas Bailey Aldrich

Richard hesitated.

"Of course I don't press you," said Mr. Perkins, with some stiffness. "You are not on the witness stand."

"I began to think I was - in the prisoner's dock," answered Richard, smiling ruefully. "However, I have nothing to conceal. I hesitated to reply to you because it was painful for me to reflect that the last time I saw my cousin we parted in anger. He charge me with attempting to overreach him, and I left the house in indignation."

"That was the last time you saw him?"

"The last time I saw him alive."

"Was there any communication between you two after that?"

"No."

"None whatever?"

"None."

"Are you quite positive?"

"As positive as I can be that I live and have my senses."

Lawyer Perkins pulled a black strand of hair over his forehead, and remained silent for nearly a minute.

"Mr. Shackford, are you sure that your cousin did not write a note to you on the Monday preceding the night of his death?"

"He may have written a dozen, for all I know. I only know that I never received a note or a letter from him in the whole course of my life."

"Then how do you account for the letter which has been found in your rooms in Lime Street, - a letter addressed to you by Lemuel Shackford, and requesting you to call at his house on that fatal Tuesday night?"

"I - I know nothing about it," stammered Richard. "There is no such paper!"

"It was in this office less than one hour ago," said Lawyer Perkins sternly. "It was brought here for me to identify Lemuel Shackford's handwriting. Justice Beemis has that paper!"

"Justice Beemis has it!" exclaimed Richard.

"I have nothing more to say," observed Lawyer Perkins, reaching out his hand towards the green bag, as a sign that the interview was ended. "There were other points I wished to have some light thrown on; but I have gone far enough to see that it is useless."

"What more is there?" demanded Richard in a voice that seemed to come through a fog. "I insist on knowing! You suspect me of my cousin's murder?"

"Mr. Taggett does."

"And you?"

"I am speaking of Mr. Taggett."

"Well, go on, speak of him," said Richard desperately. "What else has he discovered?"

Mr. Perkins wheeled his chair round until he faced the young man.

"He has discovered in your workshop a chisel with a peculiar break in the edge, - a deep notch in the middle of the bevel. With that chisel Lemuel Shackford was killed."

Richard gave a perceptible start, and put his hand to his head, as if a sudden confused memory had set the temples throbbing.

"A full box of safety matches," continued Mr. Perkins, in a cold, measured voice, as though he were demonstrating a mathematical problem, "contains one hundred matches. Mr. Taggett has discovered a box that contains only ninety-nine. The missing match was used that night in Welch's Court."

Richard stared at him blankly. "What can I say?" he gasped.

"Say nothing to me," returned Lawyer Perkins, hastily thrusting a handful of loose papers into the open throat of the green bag, which he garroted an instant afterwards with a thick black cord. Then he rose flurriedly from the chair. "I shall have to leave you," he said; "I've an appointment at the surrogate's."

And Lawyer Perkins passed stiffly from the apartment.

Richard lingered a moment alone in the room with his chin resting on his breast.

XXVI

There was a fire in Richard's temples as he reeled out of Lawyer Perkins's office. It was now twelve o'clock, and the streets were thronged with the motley population disgorged by the various mills and workshops. Richard felt that every eye was upon him; he was conscious of something wild in his aspect that must needs attract the attention of the passers-by. At each step he half expected the leveling of some accusing finger. The pitiless sunshine seemed to single him out and stream upon him like a calcium light. It was intolerable. He must get away from this jostling crowd, this babel of voices. What should he do, where should he go? To return to the yard and face the workmen was not to be thought of; if he went to his lodgings he would be called to dinner, and have to listen to the inane prattle of the school-master. That would be even more intolerable than this garish daylight, and these careless squads of men and women who paused in the midst of their laugh to turn and stare. Was there no spot in Stillwater where a broken man could hide himself long enough to collect his senses?

With his hands thrust convulsively into the pockets of his sack-coat, Richard turned down a narrow passage-way fringing the rear of some warehouses. As he hurried along aimlessly his fingers encountered

Thomas Bailey Aldrich

something in one of his pockets. It was the key of a new lock which had been put on the scullery door of the house in Welch's Court. Richard's heart gave a quick throb. There at least was a temporary refuge; he would go there and wait until it was time for him to surrender himself to the officers.

It appeared to Richard that he was nearly a year reaching the little back yard of the lonely house. He slipped into the scullery and locked the door, wondering if his movements had been observed since he quitted the main street. Here he drew a long breath and looked around him; then he began wandering restlessly through the rooms, of which there were five or six on the ground-floor. The furniture, the carpets, and all the sordid fixtures of the house were just as Richard had known them in his childhood. Everything was unchanged, even to the faded peacock-feather stuck over the parlor looking-glass. As he regarded the familiar objects and breathed the snuffy atmosphere peculiar to the place, the past rose so vividly before him that he would scarcely have been startled if a lean, gray old man had suddenly appeared in one of the doorways. On a peg in the front hall hung his cousin's napless beaver hat, satirically ready to be put on; in the kitchen closet a pair of ancient shoes, worn down at the heel and with taps on the toe, had all the air of intending to step forth. The shoes had been carefully blacked, but a thin skin of mould had gathered over them. They looked like Lemuel Shackford. They had taken a position habitual with him. Richard was struck by the subtile irony which lay in these inanimate things. That a man's hat should outlast the man, and have a jaunty expression of triumph! That a dead man's shoes should mimic him!

The tall eight-day clock on the landing had run down. It had stopped at twelve, and it now stood with solemnly uplifted finger, as if imposing silence on those small, unconsidered noises which commonly creep out, like mice, only at midnight. The house was full of such stealthy sounds. The stairs creaked at intervals, mysteriously, as if under the weight of some heavy person ascending. Now and then the woodwork stretched itself with a snap, as though it had grown stiff in the joints with remaining so long in one position. At times there were muffled reverberations of footfalls on the flooring overhead. Richard had a curious consciousness of not being alone, but of moving in the midst of an invisible throng of persons who elbowed him softly and breathed in his face, and vaguely impressed themselves upon him as being former occupants of the premises. This populous solitude, this silence with its busy interruptions, grew insupportable as he passed from room to room.

One chamber he did not enter, - the chamber in which his cousin's body was found that Wednesday morning. In Richard's imagination it was still lying there, white and piteous, by the hearth. He paused at the threshold and glanced in; then turned abruptly and mounted the staircase.

On gaining his old apartment in the gable, Richard seated himself on the edge of the cot-bed. His shoulders sagged down and a stupefied expression settled upon his face, but his brain was in a tumult. His own identity was become a matter of doubt to him. Was he the same Richard Shackford who had found life so sweet when he awoke that morning? IT must have been some other person who had sat by a window in the sunrise thinking of Margaret Slocum's love, - some Richard Shackford with unstained hands! This one was accused of murdering his kinsman; the weapon with which he had done it, the very match he had used to light him in the deed, were known! The victim himself had written out the accusation in black and white. Richard's brain reeled as he tried to fix his thought on Lemuel Shackford's letter. That letter! - where had it been all this while, and how did it come into Taggett's possession? Only one thing was clear to Richard in his inextricable confusion, - he was not going to be able to prove his innocence; he was a doomed man, and within the hour his shame would be published to the world. Rowland Slocum and Lawyer Perkins had already condemned him, and Margaret would condemn him when she knew all; for it was evident that up to last evening she had not been told. How did it happen that these overwhelming proofs had rolled themselves up against him? What malign influences were these at work, hurrying him on to destruction, and not leaving a single loophole of escape? Who would believe the story of his innocent ramble on the turnpike that Tuesday night? Who could doubt that he had gone directly from the Slocums' to Welch's Court, and then crept home red-handed through the deserted streets?

Richard heard the steam-whistles recalling the operatives to work, and dimly understood it was one o'clock; but after that he paid no attention to the lapse of time. It was an hour later, perhaps two hours, - Richard could not tell, - when he roused himself from his stupor, and descending the stairs passed through the kitchen into the scullery. There he halted and leaned against the sink, irresolute, as though his purpose, if he had had a purpose, were escaping him. He stood with his eyes resting listlessly on a barrel in the further corner of the apartment. It was a heavy-hooped wine-cask, in which Lemuel Shackford had been wont to keep his winter's supply of salted meat. Suddenly Richard started forward with an inarticulate cry, and at the same instant there came a loud knocking at the door behind him. The sound reverberated through the empty house, filling the place with awful echoes, - like those knocks at the gate of Macbeth's castle the night of Duncan's murder. Richard stood petrified for a second; then he hastily turned the key in the lock, and Mr. Taggett stepped into the scullery.

The two men exchanged swift glances. The bewildered air of a moment before had passed from Richard; the dullness had faded out of his eyes, leaving them the clear, alert expression they ordinarily wore. He was self-possessed, but the effort his self-possession cost him was obvious. There was a something in his face - a dilation of the nostril, a curve of the under lip - which put Mr. Taggett very much on his guard. Mr. Taggett was the first to speak.

"I've a disagreeable mission here," he said slowly, with his hand remaining on the latch of the door, which he had closed on entering. "I have a warrant for your arrest, Mr. Shackford."

"Stop a moment!" said Richard, with a glow in his eyes. "I have something to say."

"I advise you not to make any statement."

"I understand my position perfectly, Mr. Taggett, and I shall disregard the advice. After you have answered me one or two questions, I shall be quite at your service."

Thomas Bailey Aldrich

"If you insist, then."

"You were present at the examination of Thomas Blufton and William Durgin, were you not?"

"I was."

"You recollect William Durgin's testimony?"

"Most distinctly."

"He stated that the stains on his clothes were from a certain barrel, the head of which had been freshly painted red."

"I remember."

"Mr. Taggett, *the head of that barrel was painted blue!*"

XXVII

Mr. Taggett, in spite of the excellent subjection under which he held his nerves, caught his breath at these words, and a transient pallor overspread his face as he followed the pointing of Richard's finger. If William Durgin had testified falsely on that point, if he had swerved a hair's-breadth from the truth in that matter, then there was but one conclusion to be drawn from his perjury. A flash of lightning is not swifter than was Mr. Taggett's thought in grasping the situation. In an instant he saw all his carefully articulated case fall to pieces in his hands. Richard crossed the narrow room, and stood in front of him.

"Mr. Taggett, do you know why William Durgin lied? He lied because it was life or death with him! In a moment of confusion he had committed one of those simple, fatal blunders which men in his circumstances always commit. He had obliterated the spots on his clothes with red paint, when he ought to have used blue!"

"That is a very grave supposition."

"It is not a supposition," cried Richard. "The daylight is not a plainer fact."

"You are assuming too much, Mr. Shackford."

"I am assuming nothing. Durgin has convicted himself; he has fallen into a trap of his own devising. I charge him with the murder of Lemuel Shackford; I charge him with taking the chisel and the matches from my workshop, to which he had free access; and I charge him with replacing those articles in order to divert suspicion upon me. My unfortunate relations with my cousin gave color to this suspicion. The plan was an adroit plan, and has succeeded, it seems."

Mr. Taggett did not reply at once, and then very coldly: "You will pardon me for suggesting it, but it will be necessary to ascertain if this is the cask which Durgin hoped, and also if the head has not been repainted since."

"I understand what your doubt implies. It is your duty to assure yourself of these facts, and nothing can be easier. The person who packed the meat - it was probably a provision dealer named Stubbs - will of course be able to recognize his own work. The other question you can settle with a scratch of your penknife. You see. There has been only one thin coat of paint laid on, - the grain of the wood is nearly distingui- shable through it. The head is evidently new; but the cask itself is an old one. It has stood here these ten years."

Mr. Taggett bent a penetrating look on Richard. "Why did you refuse to answer the subpoena, Mr. Shackford?"

"But I haven't refused. I was on my way to Justice Beemis's office when you knocked. Perhaps I am a trifle late," added Richard, catching Mr. Taggett's distrustful glance.

"The summons said two o'clock," remarked Mr. Taggett, pressing the spring of his watch. "It is now after three."

"After three!"

"How could you neglect it, - with evidence of such presumable importance in your hands?"

"It was only a moment ago that I discovered this. I had come here from Mr. Perkins's office. Mr. Perkins had informed me of the horrible charge which was to be laid at my door. The intelligence fell upon me like a thunder-clap. I think it unsettled my reason for a while. I was unable to put two ideas together. At first he didn't believe I had killed my cousin, and presently he seemed to believe it. When I got out in the street the sidewalk lurched under my feet like the deck of a ship; everything swam before me. I don't know how I managed to reach this house, and I don't know how long I had been sitting in a room up-stairs when the recollection of the subpoena occurred to me. I was standing here dazed with despair; I saw that I was somehow caught in the toils, and that it was going to be impossible to prove my innocence. If another man had been in my position, I should have believed him guilty. I stood looking at the cask in the corner there, scarcely conscious of it; then I noticed the blue paint on the head, and then William Durgin's testimony flashed across my mind. Where is he?" cried Richard, turning swiftly. "That man should be arrested!"

"I am afraid he is gone," said Mr. Taggett, biting his lip.

"Do you mean he has fled?"

Thomas Bailey Aldrich

"If you are correct - he has fled. He failed to answer the summons to-day, and the constable sent to look him up has been unable to find him. Durgin was in the bar-room of the tavern at eight o'clock last night; he has not been seen since."

"He was not in the yard this morning. You have let him slip through your fingers."

"So it appears, for the moment."

"You still doubt me, Mr. Taggett?"

"I don't let persons slip through my fingers."

Richard curbed an impatient rejoinder, and said quietly, "William Durgin had an accomplice."

Mr. Taggett flushed, as if Richard had read his secret thought. Durgin's flight, if he really had fled, had suggested a fresh possibility to Mr. Taggett. What if Durgin were merely the pliant instrument of the cleverer man who was now using him as a shield? This reflection was precisely in Mr. Taggett's line. In absconding Durgin had not only secured his own personal safety, but had exonerated his accomplice. It was a desperate step to take, but it was a skillful one.

"He had an accomplice?" repeated Mr. Taggett, after a moment. "Who was it?"

"Torrini!"

"The man who was hurt the other day?"

"Yes."

"You have grounds for your assertion?"

"He and Durgin were intimate, and have been much together lately. I sat up with Torrini the night before last; he acted and talked very strangely; the man was out of his head part of the time, but now, as I think it over, I am convinced that he had this matter on his mind, and was hinting at it. I believe he would have made disclosures if I had urged him a little. He was evidently in great dread of a visit from some person, and that person was Durgin. Torrini ought to be questioned without delay; he is very low, and may die at any moment. He is lying in a house at the further end of the town. If it is not imperative that I should report myself to Justice Beemis, we had better go there at once."

Mr. Taggett, who had been standing with his head half bowed, lifted it quickly as he asked the question, "Why did you withhold Lemuel Shackford's letter?"

"It was never in my possession, Mr. Taggett," said Richard, starting. "That paper is something I cannot explain at present. I can hardly believe in its existence, though Mr. Perkins declares that he has had it in his hands, and it would be impossible for him to make a mistake in my cousin's writing."

"The letter was found in your lodgings."

"So I was told. I don't understand it."

"That explanation will not satisfy the prosecuting attorney."

"I have only one theory about it," said Richard slowly.

"What is that?"

"I prefer not to state it now. I wish to stop at my boarding-house on the way to Torrini's; it will not be out of our course."

Mr. Taggett gave silent acquiescence to this. Richard opened the scullery door, and the two passed into the court. Neither spoke until they reached Lime Street. Mrs. Spooner herself answered Richard's ring, for he had purposely dispensed with the use of his pass-key.

"I wanted to see you a moment, Mrs. Spooner," said Richard, making no motion to enter the hall. "Thanks, we will not come in. I merely desire to ask you a question. Were you at home all day on that Monday immediately preceding my cousin's death?"

"No," replied Mrs. Spooner wonderingly, with her hand still resting on the knob. "I wasn't at home at all. I spent the day and part of the night with my daughter Maria Ann at South Millville. It was a boy," added Mrs. Spooner, quite irrelevantly, smoothing her ample apron with the disengaged hand.

"Then Janet was at home," said Richard. "Call Janet."

A trim, intelligent-looking Nova Scotia girl was summoned from the basement kitchen.

"Janet," said Richard, "do you remember the day, about three weeks ago, that Mrs. Spooner was absent at South Millville?"

"Yes," replied the girl, without hesitation. "It was the day before" - and then she stopped.

"Exactly; it was the day before my cousin was killed. Now I want you to recollect whether any letter or note or written message of any description was left for me at this house on that day."

Janet reflected. "I think there was, Mr. Richard, - a bit of paper like."

Mr. Taggett riveted his eyes on the girl.

"Who brought the paper?" demanded Richard.

"It was one of the Murphy boys, I think."

"Did you hand it to me?"

"No, Mr. Richard, you had gone out. It was just after breakfast."

"You gave it to me when I came home to dinner, then?"

"No," returned Janet, becoming confused with a dim perception that something had gone wrong and she was committing herself.

"I remember, I didn't come home. I dined at the Slocums'. What did you do with that paper?"

"I put it on the table in your room up-stairs."

Mr. Taggett's eyes gleamed a little at this.

"And that is all you can say about it?" inquired Richard, with a fallen countenance.

Janet reflected. She reflected a long while this time. "No, Mr. Shackford: an hour or so afterwards, when I went up to do the chamber-work, I saw that the wind had blow the paper off of the table. I picked up the note and put it back; but the wind blew it off again."

"What then?"

"Then I shut up the note in one of the big books, meaning to tell you of it, and - and I forgot it! Oh, Mr. Richard, have I done something dreadful?"

"Dreadful!" cried Richard. "Janet, I could hug you!"

"Oh, Mr. Richard," said Janet with a little coquettish movement natural to every feminine thing, bird, flower, or human being, "you've always such a pleasant way with you."

Then there was a moment of dead silence. Mr. Spooner saw that the matter, whatever it was, was settled.

"You needn't wait, Janet!" she said, with a severe, mystified air.

"We are greatly obliged to you, Mr. Spooner, not to mention Janet," said Richard; "and if Mr. Taggett has no questions to ask we will not detain you."

Mrs. Spooner turned her small amiable orbs on Richard's companion. That silent little man Mr. Taggett! "He doesn't look like much," was the landlady's unuttered reflection; and indeed he did not present a spirited appearance. Nevertheless Mrs. Spooner followed him down the street with her curious gaze until he and Richard passed out of sight.

Neither Richard nor Mr. Taggett was disposed to converse as they wended their way to Mitchell's Alley. Richard's ire was slowly kindling at the shameful light in which he had been placed by Mr. Taggett, and Mr. Taggett was striving with only partial success to reconcile himself to the idea of young Shackford's innocence. Young Shackford's innocence was a very awkward thing for Mr. Taggett, for he had irretrievably committed himself at head-quarters. With Richard's latent ire was mingled a feeling of profound gratitude.

"The Lord was on my side," he said presently.

"He was on your side, as you remark; and when the Lord is on a man's side a detective necessarily comes out second best."

"Really, Mr. Taggett," said Richard, smiling, "that is a handsome admission on your part."

"I mean, sir," replied the latter, slightly nettled, "that it sometimes seems as if the Lord himself took charge of a case."

"Certainly you are entitled to the credit of going to the bottom of this one."

"I have skillfully and laboriously damaged my reputation, Mr. Shackford."

Mr. Taggett said this with so heavy an air that Richard felt a stir of sympathy in his bosom.

"I am very sorry," he said good-naturedly.

" No, I beg of you!" exclaimed Mr. Taggett. "Any

expression of friendliness from you would finish me! For nearly ten days I have looked upon you as a most cruel and consummate villain."

"I know," said Richard. "I must be quite a disappointment to you, in a small way."

Mr. Taggett laughed in spite of himself. "I hope I don't take a morbid view of it," he said. A few steps further on he relaxed his gait. "We have taken the Hennessey girl into custody. Do you imagine she was concerned?"

"Have you questioned her?"

"Yes; she denies everything, except that she told Durgin you had quarreled with the old gentleman."

"I think Mary Hennessey an honest girl. She's little more than a child. I doubt if she knew anything whatever. Durgin was much too shrewd to trust her, I fancy."

As the speakers struck into the principal street, through the lower and busier end of which they were obliged to pass, Mr. Taggett caused a sensation. The drivers of carts and the pedestrians on both sidewalks stopped and looked at him. The part he had played in Slocum's Yard was now an open secret, and had produced an excitement that was not confined to the clientèle of Snelling's bar-room. It was known that William Durgin had disappeared, and tdhat the constables were searching for him. The air was thick with flying projectures, but none of them precisely hit the mark. One rumor there was which seemed almost like a piece of poetical justice, - a whisper to the effect that Rowland Slocum was suspected of being in some way mixed up with the murder. The fact that Lawyer Perkins, with his green bag streaming in the wind, so to speak, had been seen darting into Mr. Slocum's private residence at two o'clock that afternoon was sufficient to give birth to the horrible legend.

"Mitchell's Alley," said Mr. Taggett, thrusting his arm through Richard's, and hurrying on the escape the Stillwater gaze. "You went there directly from the station the night you got home."

"How did you know that?"

"I was told by a fellow-traveler of yours, - and a friend of mine."

"By Jove! Did it ever strike you, Mr. Taggett, that there is such a thing as being too clever?"

"It has occurred to me recently."

"Here is the house."

Two sallow-skinned children, with wide, wistful black eyes, who were sitting on the stone step, shyly crowded themselves together against the door-jamb to make passage-way for Richard and Mr. Taggett. Then the two pairs of eyes veered round inquiringly, and followed the strangers up the broken staircase and saw one of them knock at the door which faced the building.

Richard's hasty tap bringing no response, he lifted the latch without further ceremony and stepped into the chamber, Mr. Taggett a pace or two behind him. The figure of Father O'Meara slowly rising from a kneeling

272   Thomas Bailey Aldrich

posture at the bedside was the first object that met their eyes; the second was Torrini's placid face, turned a little on the pillow; the third was Brigida sitting at the foot of the bed, motionless, with her arms wrapped in her apron.

"He is dead," said the priest softly, advancing a step towards Richard. "You are too late. He wanted to see you, Mr. Shackford, but you were not to be found."

Richard sent a swift glance over the priest's shoulder. "He wanted to tell me what part he had played in my cousin's murder?" said Richard.

"God forbid! the wretched man had many a sin on his soul, but not that."

"Not that!"

"No; he had no hand in it, - no more than you or I. His fault was that he concealed his knowledge of the deed after it was done. He did not even suspect who committed the crime until two days' afterwards, when William Durgin" -

Richard's eyes lighted up as they encountered Mr. Taggett's. The priest mistook the significance of the glances.

"No," said Father O'Meara, indicating Brigida with a quick motion of his head, "the poor soul does not understand a word. But even if she did, I should have to speak of these matters here and now, while they are fresh in my mind. I am obeying the solemn injunctions of the dead. Two days after the murder William Durgin came to Torrini and confessed the deed, offering to share with him a large sum in gold and notes if he would hide the money temporarily. Torrini agreed to do so. Later Durgin confided to him his plan of turning suspicion upon you, Mr. Shackford; indeed, of directly charging you with the murder, if the worst came to the worst. Torrini agreed to that also, because of some real or fancied injury at your hands. It seems that the implement which Durgin had employed in forcing the scullery door - the implement which he afterwards used so mercilessly - had been stolen from your workshop. The next morning Durgin put the tool back in its place, not knowing what other disposition to make of it, and it was then that the idea of shouldering the crime upon you entered his wicked heart. According to Torrini, Durgin did not intend to harm the old gentleman, but simply to rob him. The unfortunate man was awakened by the noise Durgin made in breaking open the safe, and rushed in to his doom. Having then no fear of interruption, Durgin leisurely ransacked the house. How he came across the will, and destroyed it with the idea that he was putting the estate out of your possession - this and other details I shall give you by and by."

Father O'Meara paused a moment. "After the accident at the mill and the conviction that he was not to recover, Torrini's conscience began to prick him. When he reflected on Miss Slocum's kindness to his family during the strike, when he now saw her saving his wife and children from absolute starvation, he was nearly ready to break the oath with which he had bound himself to William Durgin. Curiously enough, this man, so reckless in many things, held his pledged word sacred. Meanwhile his wavering condition became apparent to Durgin, who grew alarmed, and demanded the stolen property. Torrini refused to give it up; even his own bitter necessities had not tempted him to touch a penny of it. For the last three days he was in deadly terror lest Durgin should wrest the money from him by force. The poor woman, here, knows nothing of all this. It was her presence, however, which probably prevented Durgin from proceeding to extremities with Torrini, who took care never to be left alone."

"I recollect," said Richard, "the night I watched with him he was constantly expecting some one. I supposed him to be wandering in his mind."

"He was expecting Durgin, though Torrini had every reason for believing that he had fled."

Mr. Taggett leaned forward, and asked, "When did he go, - and where?"

"He was too cunning to confide his plans to Torrini. Three nights ago Durgin came here and begged for a portion of the bank-note; previously he had reclaimed the whole sum; he said the place was growing too warm for him, and that he had made up his mind to leave. But Torrini held on to the money, having resolved that it should be restored intact to you. He promised Durgin, however, to keep his flight secret for three or four days, at the end of which time Torrini meant to reveal all to me at confession. The night you sat with him, Mr. Shackford, he was near breaking his promise; your kindness was coals of fire on his head. His agony, lest he should die or lose his senses before he could make known the full depth of Durgin's villainy, must have been something terrible. This is the substance of what the poor creature begged me to say to you with his dying regrets. The money is hidden somewhere under the mattress, I believe. A better man than Torrini would have spent some of it," added Father O'Meara, waving a sort of benediction in the direction of the bed.

Richard did not speak for a moment or two. The wretchedness and grimness of it all smote him to the heart. When he looked up Mr. Taggett was gone, and the priest was gently drawing the coverlet over Torrini's face.

Richard approached Father O'Meara and said: "When the money is found, please take charge of it, and see that every decent arrangement is made. I mean, spare nothing. I am a Protestant, but I believe in any man's prayers when they are not addressed to a heathen image. I promised Torrini to send his wife and children to Italy. This pitiful, miserable gold, which cost so dear and is worth so little, shall be made to do that much good, at least."

As Richard was speaking, a light footfall sounded on the staircase outside; then the door, which stood ajar, was softly pushed open, and Margaret paused on the threshold. At the rustle of her dress Richard turned, and hastened towards her.

"It is all over," he said softly, laying his finger on his lip. Father O'Meara was again kneeling by the bedside.

"Let us go now," whispered Richard to Margaret. It seemed fit that they should leave the living and the dead to the murmured prayers and solemn ministration of the kindly priest. Such later services as Margaret could render to the bereaved woman were not to be wanting.

At the foot of the stairs Richard Shackford halted abruptly, and, oblivious of the two children who were softly chattering together in the doorway, caught Margaret's hand in his.

"Margaret, Torrini has made a confession that sets at rest all question of my cousin's death."

"Do you mean that he" - Margaret faltered, and left the sentence unfinished.

"No; it was William Durgin, God forgive him!"

"William Durgin!" The young girl's fingers closed nervously on Richard's as she echoed the name, and she began trembling. "That - that is stranger yet!"

"I will tell you everything when we get home; this is no time or place; but one thing I must ask you now and here. When you sat with me last night were you aware that Mr. Taggett firmly believed it was I who had killed Lemuel Shackford?"

"Yes," said Margaret.

"That is all I care to know!" cried Richard; "that consoles me!" and the two pairs of great inquisitive eyes looking up from the stone step saw the signorina standing quite mute and colorless with the strange gentleman's arms around her. And the signorina was smiling!

XXVIII

One June Morning, precisely a year from that morning
when the reader first saw the daylight breaking upon
Stillwater, several workmen with ladders and hammers
were putting up a freshly painted sign over the gate of
the marble yard. Mr. Slocum and Richard stood on the
opposite curbstone, to which they had retired in order
to take in the general effect. The new sign read, -
Slocum & Shackford. Richard protested against the
displacement of its weather-stained predecessor; it
seemed to him an act little short of vandalism; but Mr.
Slocum was obstinate, and would have it done. He was
secretly atoning for a deep injustice, into which
Richard had been at once too sensitive and too wise
closely to inquire. If Mr. Slocum had harbored a
temporary doubt of him Richard did not care to know
it; it was quite enough to suspect the fact. His
sufficient recompense was that Margaret had not
doubted. They had now been married six months. The
shadow of the tragedy in Welch's Court had long
ceased to oppress them; it had vanished with the hasty
departure of Mr. Taggett. Neither he nor William
Durgin was ever seen again in the flesh in Stillwater;
but they both still led, and will probably continue for
years to lead, a sort of phantasmal, legendary life in
Snelling's bar-room. Durgin in his flight had left no
traces. From time to time, as the months rolled on, a
misty rumor was blown to the town of his having been

seen in some remote foreign city, - now in one place, and now in another, always on the point of departing, self-pursued like the Wandering Jew; but nothing authentic. His after-fate was to be a sealed book in Stillwater.

"I really wish you had let the old sign stand," said Richard, as the carpenters removed the ladders. "The yard can never be anything but Slocum's Yard."

"It looks remarkably well up thee," replied Mr. Slocum, shading his eyes critically with one hand. "You object to the change, but for my part I don't object to changes. I trust I may live to see the day when even this sign will have to be altered to - Slocum, Shackford & Son. How would you like that?"

"I can't say," returned Richard laughing, as they passed into the yard together. "I should first have to talk it over - with the son!"

Choose from Thousands of 1stWorldLibrary Classics By

Adolphus WilliamWard
Aesop
Agatha Christie
Alexander Aaronsohn
Alexander Kielland
Alexandre Dumas
Alfred Gatty
Alfred Ollivant
Alice Duer Miller
Alice Turner Curtis
Alice Dunbar
Ambrose Bierce
Amelia E. Barr
Andrew Lang
Andrew McFarland Davis
Anna Sewell
Annie Besant
Annie Hamilton Donnell
Annie Payson Call
Anton Chekhov
Arnold Bennett
Arthur Conan Doyle
Arthur Ransome
Atticus
B. M. Bower
Basil King
Bayard Taylor
Ben Macomber
Booth Tarkington
Bram Stoker
C. Collodi
C. E. Orr
C. M. Ingleby
Carolyn Wells
Catherine Parr Traill
Charles A. Eastman
Charles Dickens
Charles Dudley Warner
Charles Farrar Browne
Charles Ives
Charles Kingsley
Charles Lathrop Pack
Charles Whibley
Charles Willing Beale
Charlotte M. Braeme
Charlotte M.Yonge
Clair W. Hayes
Clarence Day Jr.
Clarence E. Mulford

Clemence Housman
Confucius
Cornelis DeWitt Wilcox
Cyril Burleigh
D. H. Lawrence
Daniel Defoe
David Garnett
Don Carlos Janes
Donald Keyhole
Dorothy Kilner
Dougan Clark
E. Nesbit
E.P.Roe
E. Phillips Oppenheim
Edgar Allan Poe
Edgar Rice Burroughs
Edith Wharton
Edward J. O'Biren
John Cournos
Edwin L. Arnold
Eleanor Atkins
Elizabeth Cleghorn
Gaskell
Elizabeth Von Arnim
Ellem Key
Emily Dickinson
Erasmus W. Jones
Ernie Howard Pie
Ethel Turner
Ethel Watts Mumford
Eugenie Foa
Eugene Wood
Evelyn Everett-Green
Everard Cotes
F. J. Cross
Federick Austin Ogg
Ferdinand Ossendowski
Francis Bacon
Francis Darwin
Frances Hodgson Burnett
Frank Gee Patchin
Frank Harris
Frank Jewett Mather
Frank L. Packard
Frederick Trevor Hill
Frederick Winslow Taylor
Friedrich Kerst
Friedrich Nietzsche
Fyodor Dostoyevsky

Gabrielle E. Jackson
Garrett P. Serviss
Gaston Leroux
George Ade
Geroge Bernard Shaw
George Ebers
George Eliot
George MacDonald
George Orwell
George Tucker
George W. Cable
George Wharton James
Gertrude Atherton
Grace E. King
Grant Allen
Guillermo A. Sherwell
Gulielma Zollinger
Gustav Flaubert
H. A. Cody
H. B. Irving
H. G. Wells
H. H. Munro
H. Irving Hancock
H. Rider Haggard
H. W. C. Davis
Hamilton Wright Mabie
Hans Christian Andersen
Harold Avery
Harold McGrath
Harriet Beecher Stowe
Harry Houidini
Helent Hunt Jackson
Helen Nicolay
Hendy David Thoreau
Henrik Ibsen
Henry Adams
Henry Ford
Henry Frost
Henry James
Henry Jones Ford
Henry Seton Merriman
Henry Wadsworth
Longfellow
Henry W Longfellow
Herbert A. Giles
Herbert N. Casson
Herman Hesse
Homer
Honore De Balzac

Horace Walpole
Horatio Alger, Jr.
Howard Pyle
Howard R. Garis
Hugh Lofting
Hugh Walpole
Humphry Ward
Ian Maclaren
Israel Abrahams
J.G.Austin
J. Henri Fabre
J. M. Barrie
J. Macdonald Oxley
J. S. Knowles
J. Storer Clouston
Jack London
Jacob Abbott
James Allen
James Lane Allen
James Andrews
James Baldwin
James DeMille
James Joyce
James Oliver Curwood
James Oppenheim
James Otis
Jane Austen
Jens Peter Jacobsen
Jerome K. Jerome
John Burroughs
John F. Kennedy
John Gay
John Glasworthy
John Habberton
John Joy Bell
John Milton
John Philip Sousa
Jonathan Swift
Joseph Carey
Joseph Conrad
Joseph Jacobs
Julian Hawthrone
Julies Vernes
Justin Huntly McCarthy
Kakuzo Okakura
Kenneth Grahame
Kate Langley Bosher
L. A. Abbot
L. T. Meade
L. Frank Baum
Laura Lee Hope

Laurence Housman
Leo Tolstoy
Leonid Andreyev
Lewis Carroll
Lilian Bell
Lloyd Osbourne
Louis Tracy
Louisa May Alcott
Lucy Fitch Perkins
Lucy Maud Montgomery
Lydia Miller Middleton
Lyndon Orr
M. H. Adams
Margaret E. Sangster
Margaret Vandercook
Maria Edgeworth
Maria Thompson Daviess
Mariano Azuela
Marion Polk Angellotti
Mark Overton
Mark Twain
Mary Austin
Mary Cole
Mary Rowlandson
Mary Wollstonecraft
Shelley
Max Beerbohm
Myra Kelly
Nathaniel Hawthrone
O. F. Walton
Oscar Wilde
Owen Johnson
P.G.Wodehouse
Paul and Mable Thorn
Paul G. Tomlinson
Paul Severing
Peter B. Kyne
Plato
R. Derby Holmes
R. L. Stevenson
Rabindranath Tagore
Rahul Alvares
Ralph Waldo Emmerson
Rene Descartes
Rex E. Beach
Richard Harding Davis
Richard Jefferies
Robert Barr
Robert Frost
Robert Gordon Anderson
Robert L. Drake

Robert Lansing
Robert Michael Ballantyne
Robert W. Chambers
Rosa Nouchette Carey
Ross Kay
Rudyard Kipling
Samuel B. Allison
Samuel Hopkins Adams
Sarah Bernhardt
Selma Lagerlof
Sherwood Anderson
Sigmund Freud
Standish O'Grady
Stanley Weyman
Stella Benson
Stephen Crane
Stewart Edward White
Stijn Streuvels
Swami Abhedananda
Swami Parmananda
T. S. Ackland
The Princess Der Ling
Thomas A. Janvier
Thomas A Kempis
Thomas Anderton
Thomas Bailey Aldrich
Thomas Bulfinch
Thomas De Quincey
Thomas H. Huxley
Thomas Hardy
Thomas More
Thornton W. Burgess
U. S. Grant
Valentine Williams
Victor Appleton
Virginia Woolf
Walter Scott
Washington Irving
Wilbur Lawton
Wilkie Collins
Willa Cather
Willard F. Baker
William Makepeace
Thackeray
William W. Walter
Winston Churchill
Yei Theodora Ozaki
Young E. Allison
Zane Grey